WHAT OUR MINDS ONCE WERE

stories

Joe Baldwin

Contents

Viral

"…Our own personal beings are sacred. Our own lives are built by individuality, and successes are granted to the ones who fight for that right. What I have presented does not affect our own persons. It does not affect the way we view one another. What it does is open a door to a world. A new world never laid upon by human eyes. A place where we can live for the first time as a united group of citizens without fear of being assaulted, robbed, and/or killed. One unity we can build from the ground up. Years from now, the world will be a safer, happier place for one and for all. God bless all citizens of this beautiful country, and God bless these United States of America."

***

Jack Holman sat with his back against a brick wall, a 9mm pistol grasped as tightly as he would his own mother if she were still around.

Newtown Credit Union had been where Jack handled his finances for the past three years. His wife was the one who converted him and pulled him from the clenched jaw that was big name banking.

Cherie, the head teller, was one of the kindest souls Jack had encountered. Blonde hair constantly pulled into a beehive. Her makeup perfectly applied.

Always telling Jack how proud she was of the cat eye style eyeliner it took her many years to perfect. Jack found it heartwarming that she could find a task that brightened her life at the age of fifty-five. Her life was filled with love from a husband, three children, and three grandchildren. Jack watched them grow by way of pictures she lovingly shoved in his face each time he made a deposit.

There were two other bankers Jack didn't communicate much with, other than showing them his adoring smile as he peeled himself away from the jabbering mouth of Cherie. It was a close, tight-knit community. The way they treated their customers was not how Jack planned to treat them today, but he had no choice.

The rear of the small brick structure held the vehicles of the credit union employees.

Jack, as he did on every visit, had walked the quarter-mile trek from his home.

The sirens in the distance sent a shiver of shock down his spine. He knew they were coming for him. Each whining tone a cry of death. Death, something Jack had prepared for.

The rear door of the credit union exploded as his foot swung the wood structure inward. Inside, he held the weapon out in front. A ski mask was an option Jack refused. The citizens were able to watch in real time anyway. He would be instantly famous for all the wrong reasons. It was the new way of the country.

"Slowly raise your hands and climb underneath your desks," Jack said in a monotone voice to the two bankers. They did as they were told.

"Cherie, open the vault and place the largest bills into a—" Jack paused and looked around. He found a garbage can by the closest banker's desk. He emptied the contents of a banana peel and a scraped clean plastic yogurt cup with one hand while the gun was still focused on Cherie with the other.

He handed the black bag to Cherie. "You know what to do."

"Why are you—" Cherie started.

"Don't ask questions. Just do it." Jack's agitation grew. He knew The Clan were close by. The singing sirens within a mile or two. "Fucking hurry."

Cherie's arms were shoving the freshly plastic-wrapped bills into the garbage bag.

Once the bag was bulky enough, Jack said, "That's enough. Hand it over."

He took the cash and headed for the door.

"You were always so nice. Why are you—"

"Because things change. Life changes," Jack said and exited the way he entered.

***

Sergeant Garcia rested his brown steel-toe work boots on the control panel when Captain Charles sauntered in.

"What do you think this is, a summer vacation in the Florida Keys?" Captain Charles said.

"Sir, no, sir," Garcia responded, bringing his feet to the carpeted floor.

"Good, because we can't afford to lose any more of our guys."

Garcia knew Charles didn't mean losing them to vacation. The things Garcia had witnessed in the past five years, both on the screens he monitored and in person, had been incomprehensible. Garcia was grateful for his position and not being equipped with a VisionTech device. Reliving the moments through normal memories was tough enough.

"How are we looking?" Charles asked.

"Good, sir. An incident in Nebraska, but it was incapacitated before it began."

"And another in Massachusetts," Officer Grant said from the chair to the right of Garcia.

"It's my job to report to the captain, not yours," Garcia said.

Captain Charles grumbled as though he didn't care three ways from Thursday who reported to him. But Garcia earned his chevron patches, and he wasn't going to let some overachiever five months removed from boot camp ruin his chances at advancement.

"What happened in Massachusetts?" Charles asked.

"It was a—"

"Some kid who wanted to be the next school shooter was locking and loading. The Clan were there before it got anywhere," Grant interrupted.

"Great job. Keep it up," Charles said and exited. The air pressure from the door hissed their confined space tight.

"Do you ever shut up?" Garcia asked.

"We are all trying to do our best," Grant said with a shit-eating grin showing his pearly whites.

"Well, do your best when I'm not working with—"

Garcia was interrupted by an ear-splitting alarm. The thirty-foot-by-thirty-foot screen, which had the capability to show one million small boxes of footage at a time, expanded to one full screen.

"Shit. Oh, shit fuck," Garcia said.

The point of view feed rocked back and forth, showing the slide of a 9mm pistol and the location of the Newtown Credit Union.

Garcia hurried to his feet and hit the panic button. Bells blared inside their cabin and throughout the facility.

Captain Charles sped into the room. A couple of goons in full body armor stood over each of his shoulders.

"How did this get past The Enforcer?" Charles asked.

The software is not perfect, Garcia thought.

"I don't know, sir. It alerted us late." Garcia peered over at Grant, and he was quivering. Allowing an incident like this would be their heads. But Garcia remained calm and collected.

"Truck eighty-five to base. Come in, base," a voice cut into the overhead speakers.

Captain Charles grabbed the mic from the control panel. "Are you en route?"

"Yes, sir. But we are six minutes out. We won't make it in time to intercept."

"Understood. You've got eyes on them. Correct?"

"Yes, sir," the voice responded. "Got 'em up on the truck monitor."

"You will get to them. Even if the deed is done, they can still be destroyed," Charles said.

"You can count on that, Captain."

"If you need to perform Operation Sandstorm, you have my okay."

Garcia gasped, and it looked as if Grant was going to pass out.

"It shouldn't have to come to that, Cap. But thy will be done."

An ominous silence fell over the small room.

***

"Thy will be done. Really?"

Corporal Jennings shrugged while steadying the speeding Humvee through the residential streets of Newtown. "I thought it sounded dope."

"Spoiler alert, numb nuts, it didn't," Corporal Yates said.

Yates thought he knew everything. He knew the quickest route to the credit union. He knew the captain would be pissed if they ran Operation

Sandstorm too early. But what he didn't know was how to not act like an eighteen-year-old kid. He was forty-three, for fuck's sake.

"Sorry for trying to lighten the mood," Jennings said.

"Lighten the mood? What, are you gonna dim the cabin lights so we can share a three-course meal? Then make out after? How about we cook and eat the fuckstick robbing the credit union?"

"Do you have an off switch?" Jennings asked, tapping the console computer tablet.

"Yes. I won't tell you where it is, but I can give you a hint," Yates said, giving Jennings a wink.

Jennings rolled his eyes and said, "Why don't we show up at his house? We can cut him off."

"That's what the ground units are for. We are the chase unit."

"That's not what we're called."

"We should be because that's all we do."

"Jennings to ground unit," Jennings called into the mic.

"Go for a ground unit," a disgruntled voice responded.

"Are you in position at the assailant's home?"

"We are still eight minutes out. We got late notice." The walkie chirped silent.

"We're five minutes out from the credit union, but the assailant is already hauling ass outta there. We will intercept at the home. You can stand down," Jennings said.

"Copy that. Ground unit out."

Jennings clipped the walkie to the dashboard.

"We can't let this fucker ruin our streak. This is gonna get so many people fired," Yates said.

"CNN, FOX NEWS, and any other news outlet probably has the feed running already," Jennings said.

"Fuckers. Got nothin' to report anymore, in this country at least, so they're thirsty for blood. Their ratings are so low because nobody wants to watch the goody-two-shoes stories. They show reruns of the documentary of the planes striking the towers so the citizens can get their dicks hard from the adrenaline of death and destruction."

Jennings rarely shared the same views as Yates, but the news stations had previously hacked the VisionTech feeds to get a story for the eight o' clock nightly news or to stream on their social media pages.

"Cut a right here," Yates said.

"Why?"

"Because—" Yates flipped the screen to the passenger side and studied the glowing device. "This asshole's address is five streets north of the credit union, so we might be able to cut him off this way."

The wheels skittered as Jennings steered the large vehicle the wrong way down a one-way road.

Residents were out of their homes on this mid-summer afternoon, having heard the sirens incoming. That sound didn't come around these parts too often.

"Take a right at the end," Yates yelled.

Jennings cut the steering wheel into local traffic, but cars knew to clear a path like the red sea. When The Clan was out, trouble was brewing.

Yates swiped the touch screen and watched the live feed of the man holding a garbage bag full of money bound up front cement steps.

"He's home. Fuck," Yates said.

The front door of the home opened and as he entered, the feed went black.

"Then we break down the front door and take him in."

"We can't use VisionTech as probable cause to enter a home."

Jennings knew this to be the case. He graduated top of his class in boot camp. He wasn't suggesting.

"Do you want our reputation to take a hit? Do you want our streak of five years of zero crime and murder to come to an end? All because of some guy who robbed a bank of probably a couple thousand dollars?"

"Fuck no."

"Then we need to run Operation Sandstorm. We got the okay from the captain." Jennings's heart pumped overtime as they pulled to the front of the colonial home, racking their weapons. The place where this guy, Jack Holman, spent many years of his life raising his daughter and caring for his wife.

The tire swing hanging from the oak in the front lawn was a gentle reminder of what could be lost and forgotten within seconds if arrogance and pride got the best of them.

***

Jack rushed up the front stairs, entered, and slammed the door behind him, securing the dead bolt.

He dropped the weapon inside the bag to join the money.

"Emma, Emma, come here now," Jack said.

"What the fuck is happening?" It wasn't Emma but Paige who greeted him unkindly at the door.

"You know what. Now where is Emma?" Jack said.

"In her room where she will stay until she gets an explanation as to why her father robbed a bank. Have you lost your goddamn mind?"

Jack peered at the television where CNN showed Jack's point of view raising a gun to Cherie, her terrified, bewildered face he hadn't noticed at the time. The banner underneath read:

JACK HOLMAN WIELDS GUN AT CREDIT UNION, STEALS AN UNDETERMINED AMOUNT OF CASH.

"No. It is as clear as it's ever been. Paige, honey," he said, dropping the bag of cash and pistol to the floor and grabbing her cheeks, keeping her head facing straight to his. "I've lost my job."

Her face went flush between his hairy fingers.

"Yes. Exactly," he said.

"You can just get another one," Paige said.

The wailing sirens grew ever louder each passing second.

"There's no time for that. No time for talk, only action," he said and turned his head up the stairs. "Emma. Come down here right now."

Jack rushed to the kitchen as soft footfalls puttered down the steps. He gathered the five knives of differing varieties out of the wood block and laid them out one next to the other in a row.

"What's happening, Daddy? I'm scared," Emma said cowering behind her mother. Her straight blonde hair and one shimmering blue eye poked from behind Paige's hip. His little girl was growing up too fast.

"What's happening is The Clan are coming to our home right now. They won't be able to get inside unless I give them the okay. Which I will not do." Jack approached his daughter and knelt beside her. "I will not let anything happen to you. I promise. What I need you to do is take this bag and go to our secret spot. You remember where that is, right?"

"Jack, I—"

He held his palm to Paige without diverting his gaze from Emma.

Emma nodded.

"Good. You won't see me again. But make sure you do everything Mommy says, okay?"

Emma nodded. Her tears splashed onto the hardwood and Jack planted a wet kiss on her forehead.

"Jack. There are so many things we can— could've done. We could've gotten new jobs. I wish you would have talked to me."

"It wasn't possible in the allotted time. And I refuse to become one of those…"

The Humvee pulled up outside. The car door shut, and boots marched up to their front door.

A knock.

"Daddy, please."

"Do as I say. Now," Jack said.

Emma dragged the heavy bag through the living room, through the kitchen, and down the basement stairs. The money and gun thudded each step of its descent.

"You can't just leave her—"

"I can, Paige, and I will. It's our lifesaver. Our plan since this all started. Run away and start a new life in a new place."

"We could have…" Paige didn't know what they could have done differently than what Jack had done.

"This. This is the only way. I can't stand being a mouse trapped in a maze with no way to the cheese. An experiment on the people of this country. I can't stand being monitored by dignitaries and my every move being controlled. In a few weeks, Emma turns ten. I don't want her to be a part of this. I can't have her be a part of this."

Paige wrapped her arms around Jack's large shoulders.

Another knock at the door, this one more impatient than the last. "Jack Holman. We know you are inside. Come out with your hands up and we can leave your family alone," a voice from the outside called.

"Go," Jack whispered into his wife's neck. "I did all that work down there, somebody's gotta use it."

Paige nodded, wiping her snot on Jack's shirt. Something she had done on their first date. At the Newtown movie theater, the rom-com had made her sob, and she said Jack holding her that day felt like he had held her a million times before.

And now, what must be their millionth embrace would be their last.

"Last chance, Jack Holman," a new voice called. At least two Clan members, Jack noted in his head.

Jack slid a hand to her cheek, rubbing it gingerly. Then he pressed his lips to hers.

They didn't need to say *I love you*s.

Love was a feeling, not a word.

Paige was gone. Emma was gone. They would march through the basement and under the city streets within the next hour. The Clan wouldn't be able to track Paige. They would try, but—

A heart-pounding thud shook the home, and the front door was obliterated. Jack was caught off guard. They made an unlawful entry. But they should know, they were the law.

Jack rushed to the kitchen and slid behind the center island. The wood cabinets and granite countertops were no match for the weaponry The Clan carried, but he had no other option.

"Come out with your hands up, motherfucker," one of the men commanded.

Jack knew his options: 1) go with them to the facility or 2) go down in a fight he would surely lose.

He raised his arms, showing he had no weapons.

"Step out from behind the counter," the probable nicer man with the gun said.

Jack shook his head, ignoring their demands.

The shorter one holstered his gun and approached Jack while the other kept his weapon trained on him.

When The Clan member went to pull his arm down to place him in cuffs, Jack swiped one of the knives he had laid out and sliced the thigh of the heavily armored man. The short man dropped to the floor to be level with Jack, seconds before a round whizzed by and crashed through the kitchen window. He wondered if Mrs. Wilson had been struck in the crossfire while she sat in her recliner knitting.

The bleeding man unholstered his gun, but Jack was quicker. He swiped it from his hand and turned it on him. His partner crested the center island with his assault rifle leading the way.

"Please just come with us." The taller man's voice dripped with sorrow. Opposite from the aggressive manner upon entry.

Jack was so taken aback by his kindness that his arm dropped to his side.

The man with the injured leg scooted back to allow his partner to take Jack away.

Jack had other plans.

Jack knew what was best for his family.

Jack knew what was best for the country.

Jack stood and ran for the door. Gun still in hand.

When the door swung open, he was greeted by a barrage of Humvees and news vans. Cameras from local stations and cell phones pointed at him.

As he exited his home, the major networks and all of VisionTech returned to the regularly scheduled live feed of Jack Holman's point of view.

The VisionTech viewers couldn't see the impact, but it was felt when the faces of news anchors, citizens, and bystanders' faces went rigid, and Jack Holman's private broadcast went dark with one loud bang.

For those struggling to stay afloat.

There's Someone at Your Door

Friday night was movie night at the Wexler household. It was a tradition that began a year ago. Mandy popped the popcorn and Dave picked the movie. Then, the following Friday, they would switch tasks. It was fair and even. Dave enjoyed horror movies and Mandy hated them, but she endured them every other week. Just as Dave hated rom-coms but endured them for his wife. Though Mandy mentioned often that he secretly loved them, Dave vehemently denied those allegations.

This Friday, it was Dave's turn to choose the film. In the past weeks, Mandy said his options were getting weaker. She said she hadn't been truly scared of his picks the past few times, other than some cheap jump scares. So, as Mandy was sprinkling garlic powder and salt on the popcorn, he scoured the internet for the scariest movies of all time.

He chose *The Strangers*. Mandy was terrified of home invasion stories, and he knew that well. But she challenged Dave, and he had to follow through.

He started the movie before she came back from the kitchen.

"Hey, you can't start without me. It's against the rules," she said, entering the bedroom.

"You were taking too long," he said.

She sat on the bed.

"Aren't you forgetting something?" he said.

She peered around the room and shook her head.

Dave nodded at the bedside lamp.

"No," she said. "We always leave the light on during your picks."

"My movie choice means my lighting choice."

Mandy rolled her eyes, clicked the light off, placed the popcorn between their snuggling bodies as the movie began.

The glowing television was the only light in the house. It made the movie seem real. Too real.

As the masked assailants barged inside, Mandy squealed when their phones buzzed simultaneously. When they received notifications at the same time, it meant one thing.

Mandy reached for her phone, and Dave pulled her back. The remaining kernels spilled on the bedsheets.

"Ah, shoot," Mandy said.

Instead of attempting to clean, she swiped her phone.

"Motion at the front door," she said.

Dave wasn't worried since the doorbell camera picked up the neighbors exiting their driveway, or somebody utilizing the end of the cul de sac to turn around.

The buzz came again, and this time Dave paused the movie and checked his own phone.

The notification read: *There is someone at your front door.*

Somebody had rung the doorbell.

Before he could open the app to see who was there, Mandy asked, "Do you know who that is?"

She handed him the live video feed of an older man in a blue dress shirt and corduroys. He must've been in his seventies, and his nearly nonexistent hairline and deeply lined face attested to that observation.

"No." Dave felt a pain deep in his gut.

"Where are you going?" she asked.

"Getting a closer look."

Dave went across the hall and peeked through the empty bedroom window that faced the front yard. On the front stoop, the pudgy man was studying the door, willing it open.

Then a glance.

The man saw him. He didn't duck away in time.

"I think he saw me," Dave whispered.

"How do you know?"

Three raps on the door confirmed the suspicion.

"What do we do?" Mandy asked.

"I don't know. Wait for him to leave, I guess," Dave said.

"What if he doesn't leave?"

Dave remained silent. He didn't know how to answer that.

Another three knocks sounded louder that time.

"What does he want?" she said.

"I'll ask him." Dave marched to the foyer, but Mandy pulled him back.

"He could have a gun or any weapon," she said.

"You're just paranoid from the movie. I'll open the door a crack. If I talk to him, maybe he'll leave."

"Why don't we just call the police? They can talk to him."

"Mandy, he's an old man who looks out of shape. He's of no danger to us." Dave's tone came out stronger than he intended.

He pulled the handle down and opened the door a sliver. They hadn't gotten around to a storm door just yet.

"How can I help you?" Dave said. He could feel Mandy clinging to the back of his shirt.

The man looked at him with sorrowful eyes. "Does Sue Marsh live here?"

Dave was ready to deny him instantly, but the name rang a bell.

She was the woman who lived here previously. They had lived in the house for a few months, so they continued to receive Sue's mail periodically.

"No, she no longer lives here. Sorry," Dave said.

They were informed by the neighbor across the way that Sue had died inside the home, but Dave felt he didn't need to release those details.

The old man said nothing further. He briefly looked at the sky as though he were in great agony. As if Dave had driven a steel pick straight through his heart. The man turned, walked up the path, climbed into his Jeep, and drove off.

Dave closed the door and hadn't realized he was holding his breath.

He exhaled. "Well. That's that."

Dave believed that was the last he would see of the old man.

But beliefs were born from fairy tales.

***

The weekend, as it typically did, went by in a flash. Dave's mother used to say, when summer vacation came around during the school years, *"Don't blink or you'll miss it,"* and now, with summer vacation a thing of the far past, weekends had the same feeling.

Meetings, meetings about the next meeting, and lunches were the flow of the workday for Dave. When he received the job as a consultant for an advertising firm, he was ecstatic. Then, he realized the workload of the job. If he knew he would have his ear glued to a phone for most of the day, with other agencies re-directing his calls fifteen times before they hung up on him, he may have reconsidered. But the pay was great, and the hours were on par with the normal 9 to 5.

In his third meeting of the day, which gave his ear and head a break, his phone vibrated in his pocket. Mandy worked at a daycare, so she had the freedom to send a text whenever she wasn't wrangling the kids for a nap or trying to get them to eat their lunch.

Phil, Dave's boss, was too deep into his presentation to care about what the ten consultants at the long meeting table were doing. On one occasion, one of the consultants slept through one of Phil's entire presentations. The group placed bets on how long it would take Phil to notice the drooling dreamer. They all lost, as he had woken moments before Phil turned and asked if there were any questions.

Dave pulled the phone from his pocket and viewed the screen, keeping the device under the table. It was the doorbell app. There was motion at the front door. It was lunchtime, and it could have been anything. A car turning around, a neighbor going for a walk, or a package for Mandy the Amazon queen.

When he tapped to see the live view, it stole his breathing for a moment. He wondered if his sharp gasp could be heard by anyone in the conference room. When he looked up, he expected Phil to be staring at him like a teacher scolding a student for using a phone during class. But Phil was droning on about the numbers they pulled for the quarter. Something that could've been sent in an email.

He watched as a mac-and-cheese-colored Jeep sat beyond the partially green grass, sitting in the road and blocking his driveway. It was the same Jeep he watched the old man drive off in on Friday night. The circle eyeballs were staring at Dave as though the headlights were going to steal his soul.

Before he could tell Mandy, a text from her came through.

Is that the same guy from Friday?!

He responded, *I think so.*

What was this guy doing? What did he want? Dave had answered his burning question. But it wasn't enough for this guy. What was his connection to Sue Marsh? If he knew the name, he had to have known her. Maybe she was an old friend or girlfriend he hadn't realized passed on? If he told him she no longer lived there, then he should have moved on.

Oh my god! He's pacing outside his car, Mandy texted.

Dave viewed the live feed and sure enough, he was pacing, and his arms were flailing like he was conversating with himself.

It was growing ever more tense, and Dave feared he would start trying doors and windows to search for his deceased friend.

"If you'll excuse me," Dave said and exited the room.

Dave needed to get outside and think of the best course of action.

He called Mandy.

"What do we do?" she said after one ring. She sounded out of breath and panicky.

"We take a moment to breathe."

"Breathe? There's a man outside our house. I can't breathe until he's gone," she said.

"Okay, okay. It looks like he's not leaving until he gets the answers he needs, and I have three more hours of work."

"He might do something in that time," she said.

"I know. I'll call the police non-emergency number and I'm sure they can get somebody out there. We live in a quiet town."

Dave could tell she was relaxing a bit. "Okay. I think that's best."

"Okay. I love you."

"Love you."

Dave hung up and phoned the police department.

"Fairview Police," a grumbly woman said.

He explained the situation to the dispatcher.

"Sir, we already have an officer on the way to that address."

Dave was silenced. "Really?"

"Yes, sir. Two minutes out."

"Oh, okay. Thank you."

He hung up and realized his retired neighbors across the way must've called on their behalf.

Thank the Lord for good, observant neighbors.

***

In the week following the incident, there were no more incidents. Nobody showing up unwanted. Nobody cruising by in strange vehicles. But each time that doorbell app rang to notify them of movement, Mandy would interrupt anything to check the cause immediately.

They found out from the police that his name was Steven Marsh, and his mother was Sue Marsh. Sue had died ten years ago. Dave hadn't realized it was that long ago when the neighbor was speaking about her. Steven had showed up looking for his mother. He knew she was dead, but in his mind, she was still living and breathing in the home Dave and Mandy purchased. A personal and spiritual connection to the dwelling.

"I don't want to live here anymore," Mandy said to Dave now.

"You're overreacting," Dave said, sipping his morning coffee.

"Are you kidding me? We don't know how psychotic he is. He could have wanted to see his dead mother so badly that he broke down the front door and did God knows what."

Dave sighed and shook his head. "He's just a confused old man. Maybe he was off his meds for those days he visited."

"Exactly. When people are off their normal medication schedule, they are capable of anything."

Dave had had enough of this weeklong paranoid session. The man was gone. He was taken to the hospital and evaluated. The officer assured Dave they would keep a close eye on him after a mental break like the one he experienced.

"Just drop it. He is not coming back. Get over it," Dave said. The forceful nature of his response shocked even himself.

Mandy reacted in the worst way possible. She didn't yell. She didn't strike Dave. She didn't even give him a nasty look. She simply remained silent and left the house for work. That scared Dave. When she was silent, she was deadly.

***

Fridays were the slow days at work for Dave. There were few meetings, and the calls he had to make begging companies for their business were taken care of earlier in the week. Dave looked forward to getting home on Friday evenings and relaxing for the next few days. This Friday, he dreaded going home.

Mandy was already home, and when he watched the video of her entering, she looked upset. Her beautifully lined lips were turned downward. Streaks down her plump cheeks indicated she had been crying. She was frustrated when the simple task of unlocking the door didn't work for a moment. He was going to have a sit-down talk with her that he didn't want to have.

Dave decided to give her some time alone to cry it out and calm down before he got home.

Gonna be home late, he texted Mandy.

Okay was her response.

If the doorbell video wasn't enough to know she was upset, the one-word text message did the trick.

Dave exited the parking lot from work, and it usually took him eight minutes to reach home. Instead, he took a right, taking him in the opposite direction. The Ugly Duckling, the local bar, was a mile down the main road. He would have a few beers, then tame the snarling beast at home.

The one-half bar, one-half restaurant was not packed as it should be for a Friday evening. Though it was only 5:30, and he didn't know if the young kids nowadays waited until 11 to get the party started. Dave was sleeping by 11 each night. One indication out of many that he was getting old.

As the minutes ticked by into hours and one beer turned to two, and two to three, Dave was struck with a sense of uneasiness for the first time. It was eight at night and Mandy hadn't made any attempt to contact him. No text, no phone call, no smoke signals. When Dave checked his phone during what he determined to be his final drink, his phone refused to turn on. Social media scrolling and YouTube videos over the course of the slow workday had depleted the battery.

Dave paid for his tab and took the short trip home.

The beers hit him worse than he thought they would. He would consider himself buzzed, and if he was pulled over, he couldn't be certain that he could pass a sobriety test. As he turned onto the cul de sac, he realized other than a few peanuts at the bar, he hadn't eaten since noon. Mandy was good about cooking and having dinner ready when he got home.

But when he pulled up front, the lights were out in the exterior and interior of their home. Unless sleep was in the cards, she ran up the lighting bill every day. She could've slipped off to sleep he tried to convince himself. There was a possibility—until he saw the front door was ajar. *Lights on and locked up* was her motto. It was unexpected to find the house that way, and unexpected was not good. Furthermore, the doorbell camera was missing.

Dave approached the home, the place he and his newlywed wife were meant to feel safe. A place they could return to at the end of a stressful day to melt away with some rest and relaxation. It didn't feel that way now. It felt like he was stepping into someone else's home. An invasion of his own privacy.

He pressed a foot inside, and the first thing he noticed out of place was the ottoman that was for resting feet in the center of the couch and loveseat. It was on its side and moved into the foyer beside the coatrack.

"There you are," a voice said before Dave could find its source.

When he rounded the corner, the man who had visited them twice last week sat on the loveseat. The sight now forever tainted memories of making love the first day they moved in. Sitting by the fireplace with hot chocolate, having deep conversation with one another. All ruined.

The man was naked. His pale body like a blob on the cushion. His protruding stomach hung over his waist ending just before his penis. His penis rested atop his wrinkled ball sack, which dangled over the edge. He sat stoically with his fingertips touching and his gaze on the askew white rug that Mandy thought accented the mantle of tchotchkes and pictures from their past.

"What are you doing in my—"

"This home does not belong to you."

"I'm sure you have great memories—"

"You don't know what I have," the man's voice raised to an uncomfortable level.

"You're right. I don't know anything about you. Which is why you need to leave now," Dave said. What had this guy done to Mandy? Where was she?

"I was born in this room right here on the floor. My mother didn't believe in hospital birthing. Eleven pounds, twelve ounces. Can you believe that? No pain pills, no hippie spells. None of that. Just my one-of-a-kind mama."

While he was going through his past, Dave was shuffling in minor motions toward the panel on the wall. The security panel they never set to arm. A foolish move considering the current situation. But he knew there was a code that sent out an emergency signal.

"Mama was never supposed to leave this place, ya know? This was her first house. Her father built it, ya know? Him and a friend bult it from the ground up. It took them six months. That's it. Can you believe that?"

Dave didn't care if it was built by aliens in 44 AD. He wanted this lunatic removed from the home he purchased. He searched around the naked man for any weapons or objects he could use in defense. He felt silly fearing this old man, but who knew what he was capable of. But he took a chance. He turned to punch the number into the panel.

"Your wife couldn't give me an erection. Can you believe that?"

Damn the code. Damn the police. Damn it all to hell. He was going to kill this man. Legally.

"The fuck did you just say?"

"Oh. I just said your wife couldn't give me an erection. She do that for you?"

Dave's ears were pulsating with rage, so he must've not heard what the old man said correctly. Regardless, he approached him. Dave grasped his neck and planned to snap it like a rotted twig in a forest.

"You should go to her. Pleasure her. I tried, but it was like putting playdoh in a keyhole."

Dave squeezed him like he was getting the last bit of ketchup from the bottle. He could feel his Adam's apple bobbing in his palm. The old man put up no fight to get Dave off him. It was like this was his plan all along.

"I—I was," the man's words sputtered out. Dave had heard enough.

"Dave."

He released his grip and turned at the new voice in the room. It was Mandy. She had come up from the basement in the robe she wore to bed.

He was relieved to see her. He was on his way to embrace her. Make sure she wasn't harmed by the monster on the couch. He stopped when he saw the gun she was holding.

"It's over, Mands. You can put the gun down. I have this under control," Steven said.

"Why would I want to shoot my own brother?"

Dave's blood ran from his head to his feet, and a wave of dizziness overtook him.

"Wh-what do you mean?"

"I mean Steven is my older brother."

"He just tried to fuck you," Dave said bluntly.

"What? No, he didn't. Years back he started to become confused. It made him disoriented. Ever since then, I help him."

"What do you mean by that?"

"Never mind what I mean. What's important is that you are out, and he is in."

"I'm out?"

"Yes. When he showed up on our porch that day, I was so excited. He had come back home, and we would live the rest of our lives together with Mom."

"Your mom is dead. That's what the neighbor said. That's what the police said." Dave's head was swimming with questions and confusion.

Mandy released this raucous laughter, and her brother joined in from the couch. Dave felt like he was in a carnival funhouse, and they were actors trying to drive him insane. "Mom isn't dead. She's right downstairs. Come. Let me show you."

With an inviting smile, the woman he formally knew as his wife invited him to the wood paneled, eighties basement he had been in so many times since they moved in several months back.

"No. I'm not going downstairs and I'm not leaving. My name is on the mortgage. Not yours," he said, pointing to Mandy. "Not yours." He pointed to Steven. "And not your mother's."

Mandy took three large barefoot steps toward Dave and looked deep into his eyes. Like she did when they were giving their vows at the altar. Only now her eyes had a tinge of crazy mixed in with loving.

"Seeing is believing, David," she said, grabbing his hand, and guided him to the basement.

***

The creak of the steps under the heavy footfalls of first Mandy, then Dave, then Steven, led them to the carpeted 1980s basement. The laundry room door was fully open, exposing the view of dirty underwear, shirts, bras, and bedsheets piled like a flood of cloth. Rounding the corner, the space for watching TV on Dave's favorite device, the 65-inch television, was littered with debris from the wood paneled walls. Somebody, one of the siblings standing one on each side of Dave, had taken a sledgehammer to the only barrier keeping the inner workings of the home hidden.

A hole the size of a street manhole cover showed a face. What used to be a face. Its skin had melted away. Its nose had fallen off. Its mouth no longer required dentistry work. Its cheeks sunken to nonexistence. Its color a post-barbeque charcoal gray. Its face as shocked as Dave was, staring at one another.

"Is that?" Dave asked.

"Our mother. I told you she still lived here," Steven said.

"She is fucking de—"

"Don't you say it," Steven said, his face growing wearier.

"It's okay, Steven, we know she died ten years ago, but it's her spirit that remained in the house," Mandy said. "I so enjoyed coming down here when you were at work and just having day-long conversations with her. Talking about the good times and the bad times."

Dave was beginning to think he was the loony one. He was starting to think talking to your dead mother's corpse was a normal weekend activity.

"You know what. I'm just gonna go. I don't know where, but anyplace is better than this one."

As Dave moved to the stairs, Steven blocked his path. The pale bowling ball belly in his nude glory.

"I can't let you do that," Steven said.

"What—I'm not going to tell anybody about this. I don't care enough to. If you and your sister want to have a tea party, there's no need to steep my bag. Goodbye," Dave said, shoving Steven out of his way. What he forgot was Mandy still held the gun.

"Steven's right. You can't leave now."

"Are you going to force me to stay in my own home?" Dave asked.

"Nope," Mandy said and pulled the trigger.

The report was deafening and before he could blink, Dave was on the floor. The smell of gunpowder lit up his olfactory receptors, and the two bodies moving on him forced him to his feet.

"Get back here," Steven said. But Dave was at the top of the stairs before Steven finished his sentence.

Dave was out of the front door, and the neighbors across the way were outside of their house. It looked like they were ready to go in and fight with kitchen utensils against a gun. The other neighbors flicked their porch lights on and went as far as that. Curiosity often killed the human. So be curious from a distance.

Dave stood behind the couple from across the way. They were putting their lives on the line for a guy they had two short conversations with.

Thank God for good neighbors.

***

Two more gunshots rang out from the house, and Dave knew what that meant.

Mandy and Steven never exited the home.

Once the police completed their initial questioning and investigation, Dave received a call a few days later while he stayed in a hotel a town over. If the bullet fired at him had been mere inches to the right, he would with most certainty be dead rather than suffering a flesh wound. The couple across the way called and offered to put him up until he landed back on his feet, but he declined.

"Mr. Wexler, how much did you actually know about your wife?" the grizzled voice on the other line said. It was an odd way to begin a conversation.

"I don't know. Enough, I guess. We met at a bar a year and a half ago. We got married months ago and moved into that house shortly after. She had a stable job—"

"Where did she work?" the detective interrupted.

"At a daycare."

"Which one?"

"Why am I the one being interrogated?"

"No interrogations here, Mr. Wexler. It's just that your wife, ex-wife, escaped from the Fairfield Hills mental hospital two years ago. They don't go through too much trouble to hunt down escapees who aren't known to be a danger to the public."

Dave lay on the firm mattress of the perfectly made bed. The room was spinning faster than he felt his life was. The woman who seemed more normal than an ex he had who would text him three thousand times on a daily basis was the actual nutcase.

"Mr. Wexler, are you still there?"

"Yes. Sorry. I'm—just taking in the news. I had no idea."

"Sorry to be the one to tell you."

"And her brother Steven?"

"Here's the thing that's going to make this a special on nighttime television. He was staying in the same institution. Only he was released on good terms. The kicker here is they aren't brother and sister. According to Fairfield Hills, they were the best of friends inside. Apparently once they started hanging out, they improved. Or so the facility believed. When he was released, his first stop was his childhood home."

"She seemed so normal," Dave said.

"She was on her medication."

A revelation. He had seen Mandy take pills constantly, but she had an excuse each time, and Dave never questioned her. Migraine, seasonal allergies, birth control. It all seemed plausible to him.

"I wish I had known," Dave said.

The detective took a pause. "Why do you say that?"

"Because I could have gotten her help before she committed the actions she did."

The detective grunted in what sounded like agreement. "Well, Mr. Wexler, good luck with everything. And if you need anyth—"

"I've got your number," Dave said and hung up the phone.

As he lay on the hotel bed, he thought back through the past year. From meeting her in The Ugly Duckling to making love on the loveseat in front of the open front window, to her firing a gun at him. It had gone by in a flash, and the only thing he would have done differently was talk to her more. She had her moments when she would isolate, and he would ask if she was okay. She always said she was fine, but he should have pressed her.

Maybe she would still be here.

Maybe she would be sitting by her bed reading her favorite novel.

Maybe if he wasn't in his own head so much, he would have recognized the hurt in her eyes.

He was shaken from his thoughts by a hard knock on his hotel room door.

He wouldn't answer it this time.

This time was different.

For Christina, we can get through anything together.

Cold-Hearted

I'm not doing this.

The handle of the knife is grasped firmly in my hand. I watch as the blade enters and exits the chest of the woman for the thirteenth…fourteenth time. The crimson river is spurting and flowing. It covers my torso and face. It is in my eyes, one is closed, but I wipe it clear and continue.

I'm not doing this.

The ceiling in the atrium is high. The chandelier gleams above us. Pictures hang on the white walls. A man, a woman, and a child.

Is the man home? She released a scream before her mouth could be covered. It would have woken him. He would have been standing at the bottom of the marble staircase with shotgun in hand. There are several weapons on hooks above the fireplace.

Is the child home? He must be the age of ten by the looks of the photos. An age of cowardness and fear. I imagine him remaining under the covers, waiting for the bad man to leave.

I'm not doing this.

The knife I retrieved from the wood block in the kitchen is becoming useless. I feel I am reentering the same previously punctured holes. But the chest is the only place I am permitted to aerate. The woman must have died minutes ago, but I cannot stop. I want to. I want to, quite badly.

I'm not doing this.

This is not me. I have a family. A daughter the age of ten. A wife whom I love. I cannot let them see me like this. Blood everywhere. A woman I have killed. But I didn't kill her. I have lost control of my body. A lame excuse to tell the police.

I'm not doing this.

"Momma?" The boy. Just as I imagined it would happen. Only my head chose the wrong man of the house. The boy of ten stands at the bottom of the staircase with a shotgun pointed inches from my head. I should have been facing, watching the stairs. But I have no choice in the matter.

I'm not doing this.

I want to tell the boy this, but even at his naïve age, he wouldn't believe me.

"Your mom is okay." Stupid. She is not. He can see that with his own blue eyes. The same corneas as his mother.

I am given permission to cease stabbing so I can handle the boy. I stand. The barrel is at crotch level. That would hurt. I grab the gun and attempt to take it from his small hands. He pulls the trigger.

I'm not doing this.

The gun clicks.

Stupid kid doesn't know how to load a gun before using it. He loses his grip, and I am in control of the firearm now. I throw the gun down the hall. It clatters, hurting my ears. Stupid rich people and their large homes.

Do it. Hot breath whispers in my ear.

I'm not doing this.

The kid runs. He darts for the front door. Stupid kid. He slips on his mother's blood, and his head bounces off the hardwood.

I didn't do that.

Complete the ritual.

My cries for the whispers to stop have fallen silent. I try again.

Leave me alone. I'm not doing this.

Complete the ritual or I will remain within you forever.

I'm not doing this.

God, I am acting like my ten-year-old when she can't have ice cream. Tears. Whining. Feet stomping. Eventually, she got what she wanted. I will not.

I'm doing this.

***

It's done.

I walk three miles and return to my home, and the thing leaves my body in the front yard.

My mouth is forced open, and my lower abdominals burn from the movement. I am more agape than I have ever been. My jaw comes unhinged as it exits. A plume of whirling smoke jets from my insides out into the open air of my quiet neighborhood.

Anne from across the road is nosy, and she will call the police. If her heart doesn't give out from the sights and sounds.

A thing, a monster, forms from the tornado of smoke. I know the thing's voice well, but the visuals have remained a mystery. Until now.

"You've done well. I will return when the time is right," the thing bellows. A monster of a child's dream, I think. Seven feet tall. Long branch-like fingers. Legs thick as tree trunks stomp softly onto my lawn. A dark hooded cloak shadows its facial features.

"Never return. You have brought so much pain to me and my family over the past few weeks. My wife wants to leave me because of you, and she will take my daughter with her. So, please never come back." My voice is strained and burning.

Tears fall to the corners of my mouth. This monster will cause me no more pain. The murder weapon remains wrapped in a towel in my rear pocket. I have become an expert in hiding murder weapons. But it will catch up to me if this doesn't stop. If I don't make it stop.

I stab the monster. The blade enters its thick, coarse skin on the upper leg—if it can be called that.

I fall to the ground. I hear cackling laughter under the hood before I feel the pain in my quadricep. My blood is spilling from me onto the same lawn where I attempted to teach my daughter to play catch, beside the street where I let go when she found her

balance on her bicycle. No blood pours and no markings remain on the monster. It vanishes.
    Blood pours from me.
    I did this.
    All of this.

***

An article from the Greenwich Herald:

WOMAN AND CHILD SLAIN IN MURDER CONNECTED TO OTHER KILLINGS, POLICE SAY

April 23, 2019

Monica Wheeler of 2467 Hammock Drive was murdered with multiple stab wounds to the chest.

Her son whose name has not been released due to his minor status was also killed. The crime appears to be connected to a string of murders that have occurred in Greenwich over the course of the previous weeks, police say.

"We believe there are two assailants due to the nature and rapidness of which these crimes have occurred," a police spokesman said at a news conference early Tuesday morning.

"We also believe all the murders are connected. The Greenwich Police Department has come to this conclusion because of the calling card left at each crime scene. All the respective victims had their chests cracked open and their hearts removed. The organs were then subsequently placed into each victim's home freezers. These murderers must be stopped. As the crimes indicate to us, these assailants have ice-cold hearts."

Anyone with information is urged to contact the Greenwich Police Department.

For those battling a demon inside them.

ESCAPE

I escaped.

I finally did it.

The grass is greener than I imagined.

The kids are playing with shouts of joy.

Families are showing each other love, just as I have seen on the TV shows.

I am free.

I am finally free.

***

"You are talking in your sleep again."

A dream. Michael told me that the scary dreams were called nightmares. A nightmare. A happy nightmare. One where I escaped. One where my six sisters and three brothers would be released from this home.

I tug at my arm as I do every time I awake. That time could be the time Pa forgets to secure the lock. One slip-up. One mistake is all it takes.

"I had the dream again. The one where I am on the outside," I say.

"What does it look like?"

"There are houses close to each other. There is green grass in the front yards. There is a stop sign."

"What's that?"

"It's for when you are driving and you need to stop your car so other cars can go," I say.

"Oh. Are we going to get outside soon?"

"Soon. Michael says Pa will be going out for grocery day today. I will try then."

"You will get caughted," another voice in the dark chimes.

"Not if I call for help," I say.

"How will you break the chains?" the voice from the bunk below asks.

"Michael. He took a saw from Pa's workbench. When he is giving us our food, he will hide it in his shirt, then hand it to me," I say.

"Will that really work?"

"It has to. Then I will open the window and escape," I say.

The chronic coughs of lower bunk sister encapsulate the room. She is not doing well. None of us are doing well. My wrists are daintier by the day, but the chains are tied tighter. If I can't get out today, will there ever be a time when lower bunk sister gets the attention she needs?

***

"Food time," Michael says, entering with a tray of plastic plates.

A scoop of mashed potatoes. A sliver of chicken. A quarter of a biscuit.

Daily mealtime is my favorite time of day. My stomach stopped growling, and now it hurts most of the time when it needs food. The food is comforting, but Michael's face is my whole world.

"Special delivery for you," Michael says, slipping the handsaw from his rear waistband, placing it on her side and the tray of food on top. "Keep still for the check," Michael whispers.

I nod my head, peeking through the metal safety bars.

"Enjoy, all," Michael says, exiting.

I create a bridge, bending my back into an arch. The feet shackles clang against the safety bars. Pa will hear. He always hears.

Footsteps.

The clanking of the wrist chains causes the steps to rush. The saw is nearly out of reach of the tips of my fingers. A *tap, tap, tap* gets the saw where it needs to be.

The door swings open. The light from the hall illuminates the face across from me. Across the bunk, sister's emaciated arms sit atop her plate, ready to dig in.

"What's that rackus I hear in here?" Pa says.

All silent.

"What's the motherfuckin' rackus? Don't make me ask again."

"Just trying to get comfortable," I say.

"You don't get to be comfortable. You think the lord was comfortable walking through a desert for forth days and forty nights? I don't think so. Now eat up. We don't got all day."

The paper plates are soaked with grease stains of the previous day's daily food ration. Father walks with his hands in an "at rest" pose as he wanders past the three bunk beds, searching with his eyes for anything he deems to be out of place. The saw digging into my back is as unpleasant as it sounds.

"You look nervous, girl," Pa says. His sun-spotted, wrinkled gaze looms over me. The light from the hall shines on one half of his face.

"No, Pa. This is my excited face," I say.

He shows an expression that he doesn't believe me and reaches his claw hand over the safety bars and touches my exposed stomach from the shirt that stopped fitting when I received it five years ago. His hand makes a sandpapery sound and is rough on my lower abdomen.

Pa's moans mean it's time to close my eyes and count to one thousand. That's when he's finished. Always when I count to one thousand.

But the counting is not needed. Lower bunk sister begins hacking and she won't stop.

"Oh, stop that rackus coughing, girl. Get over yourself. All of yous need to get over yourselfs."

Pa exits and slams the door behind him.

"Why is he so mean all the time? We never did nothin' to him," across the bunk sister says.

Across the bunk sister is the only sister I can see. Her skull-shaped face and long tee shirt she got from Michael that says *FOO FIGHTERS* on it. I don't know what a Foo Fighter is, but I would really like a shirt that goes down to my knees. It would make me so much comfier.

"Michael says Pa didn't have a good childhood. Says he's mad he can't go back in time and do the stuff he can't do now that he's old. Michael says that why we're here. We are living his childhood dreams through him or something like that," I say.

"I'm mad," lower bunk sister says when her coughing ceases. "I'm mad I can't ever leave. I just want to leave. Go to places I see during TV time."

"Me too. And I will get you out of here. Get all of us out of here," I say.

***

It is always dark.

I don't know when the dark is outside. Michael says that people sleep when the dark is outside. When Ma and Pa sleep is when I can make noise. Not a lot of noise, but some.

I know when mealtime comes. The final meal and the first meal are ten hours apart. That must be when it's dark outside.

The chicken meal was the final mealtime. That happened a long time ago, so it is okay to make noise. It should be okay.

I arch my back and remove the saw. It is light in my hand. It is in a weird shape. Wide where I hold my hand and gets smaller on the other side. The danger part is underneath.

Pa always chains both hands to both sides of the bed. That is not comfy for me. I cannot move and that makes me cry. I just like to move. I like to sleep on my side and be able to keep an eye on across the bunk sister without hurting my turning neck. Ma used to come in some days and undo my left-hand side. She did that before she disappeared. Now Michael will do that for me. Michael taught me my left from my right. "Hold your thumb and pointer finger in the shape of an 'L'. Whichever 'L' looks right, then that is your left hand," he had said.

Michael undid my left hand today. I love Michael, but I wish Ma was still around. Ma came in and planted a wet kiss on the center of my forehead. I miss her kisses.

I hold the saw with my left and begin cutting the silver chain holding my right. The sound is quieter than I thought. A small shushing noise. It's a sound I sometimes hear coming from the outside. It sounds like somebody cutting something. I wish Pa would take the wood away from the windows so I can see the outside. I just want to see, that's all.

I can't see if it is cutting the chains or if I am cutting in the same place. My eyes can see some movements. Across the bunk sister is turning in her bunk. Michael gave me a flashlight one time, but Pa found it and took it away. When I didn't tell him where I got it, he unchained me and brought me to the dungeon room. I never want to go back there.

A door opens.

Footsteps.

I arch and tuck the saw back underneath me. It causes my chains to rattle, and I hear the whines of lower bunk sister waking. Then her coughing begins again. This will anger Pa. Especially when it's lights out time.

The footsteps stop and then move closer.

The door opens and I lay perfectly still. I hope lower bunk sister does the same. But she can't help her hacking, and I can't help her.

I keep my eyes squeezed tightly shut, and I can smell Pa standing over me.

"Come with me," Pa says. The chains rattle and I can hear the pop of the locks unlatching. I dare a look when the footsteps move away. I see Pa holding lower bunk sister's hand and leading her out of the room. The door shuts.

I fear that is the last time I will see lower bunk sister. And we will surely have a new family member by the next day.

***

The saw is not working, and I tell Michael that when he delivers first mealtime.

"Give it back. I will find something better," Michael says. I hand him the saw, and he heads for the door.

"Is lower bunk sister coming back?" I ask.

Michael frowns and looks at the floor before leaving and closing the door behind him.

"She's not coming back," across the bunk sister says. "It was the noise she was making."

"But that's not her fault," I say. Tears fall down my cheeks. "It's not fair." My voice is growing louder.

"Quiet. You don't want to go to the dungeon room," across the bunk sister says.

"I don't care anymore. I just don't care," I shout.

Footsteps return and Michael walks back in.

"What's going on?" Michael asks.

"Nothing. Just leave me be," I say, turning on my side and closing my eyes. Sleep always makes time go by fast. Maybe the faster time goes, the faster I can leave this room. "My head hurts. My head hurts real bad."

"I'll be back in just a second. I know just the thing," Michael says and whisks away.

He returns moments later with a glass. All I have ever seen here are plastic drinking containers. Never glass.

"Drink this," he says.

I take it with my left hand and the water feels so nice flowing down my throat. I drink the whole thing in a few seconds. My head feels better. It still hurts, but it's better.

"Thank you," I say.

"You're welcome," Michael says. "Now, I will see you soon for second mealtime."

"Wait," I say. Michael stands in the doorway. "Can't you get the key and unlock me? Please."

Michael says nothing and closes the door, walking away from his sisters.

I let out a frustrated growl.

I have had enough.

I pull and tug on my right-hand chain. The safety bars shake, and I can see them coming loose from the bed frame. I kick frantically with my leg, and the bar at the end begins to lift as well.

Michael rushes back into the room. "Stop that. Stop that right now," he says but does nothing to stop me.

I continue my rage until the entire safety bar comes off. It dangles from my wrist. The same happens for the smaller bar attached to my foot. I drop to the floor. The fall is far. The safety bar hits first and then my right arm lands on that. "Ow, ow, ow, ow," I scream.

"Well, you know, that's what happens when you don't listen to Pa. They are keeping you safe from the world. You don't know—"

I stop listening to Michael and scuttle out of the room.

He places his arm in front of the open doorway. "I can't I-let you g-go. Okay? So, go back to bed and Pa won't need to know what happened."

"Why?" I say, sounding more grown up than ever. "What?"

"Why do you help me try to get out, but then I get out and you won't let me leave?"

He looks confused. "Because this is where you belong. All the things I gave to you were never going to help you escape. My job is hope. I give you hope because no one person can live without hope. Jesus once said—"

I pick up the long safety bar and, with all my emaciated strength, smack Michael across the head. He goes down, and his eyes are closed. He might be dead, but I think he's just sleeping.

I walk into the TV room that I haven't seen since the last TV time a very long time ago. TV time was Ma's idea. It's a TV so big that it's bigger than me. The kitchen is always covered up during TV time. I open the refrigerator and it is stocked with food of all different kinds. There are oranges and apples on the counters. There is even a water dispenser on the fridge. I continue and there is another room with a couch and chair. And another big TV. Next to my sisters' and my bedroom is another closed door. Brothers are staying in there.

I find the front door and I need a key to get to the outside. But seeing the outside is almost enough. The curtains are blocking the outside when we are out here. The grass is just as green as I dreamed. There are people walking on the other side of the street, pushing a stroller. I bang on the window. They keep walking.

I find Ma and Pa's room. A big bed that is higher than I am. A drawer I pull out. It's got Pa's shirts and underwear. I close it and find a desk with a drawer. I open it and find three keys.

I take the keys to the front. First one doesn't work. The second one does. The door opens, and the warm air hitting my face and breathing in the fresh air makes that headache from earlier disappear.

Then a hand grabs me, pulling me back inside.

"Michael, let me go," I say, looking up at his bloodied face.

"No, you were naughty, so you go to the dungeon."

Michael carries me and my safety bar down some stairs, my kicking and screaming not helping. He places me down and shuts the door. The thunk of the lock sounds right after.

It smells down here. A stinky smell that goes into your nose and stays there for what feels like forever. It feels like having a booger of smells. There is a small window, but it is up too high. It gives me enough light to see. Brighter than inside the room. The hard floor is not as comfy as my bed, but it got hot in there, and the cool floor is nice.

I look up at the chains hanging from the walls. They are bolted into the rock wall. I walk along the sets of chains. When my eyes find the final set of chains farthest away from the door, I see a little girl suspended in the air in the shape of an "X." She is not just sleeping. All the stuff that is supposed to stay on the inside to keep you living is on the floor in front of her. I run to the other side of the room by the door and throw up.

I think I found lower bunk sister.

***

Pa is here.

Michael is behind him, entering the dungeon room.

I am curled on the floor. I think I slept because I don't remember any footsteps until they were here.

"I hear you were bad today," Pa says.

"No, you are bad, every day," I say.

Pa is shocked. "You're talkin' to me that way? Who do you think gives you food and a place to sleep? Me. Where do you think I just was? Workin'. Do you work? No, you don't. Until then, you live by my rules. Got it?"

I nod.

"Good. Michael, take her back to her room. This punishment will require thinkin' while I clean up my other mess," Pa says and nods his head in the direction of lower bunk sister.

Michael nods. "C'mon." I take his hand, the safety bar making it difficult to get up the stairs. After many failed attempts, Michael carries me. The large bandage on his forehead makes me giggle. "What's so funny?"

"Nothin'," I say.

We reach the top of the stairs, and he places me on my own two feet. The sound of the metal clanging happens before I see it. Across the bunk sister is wearing the same safety bars and clunks Michael on the head. He goes down again.

"What was that?" Pa calls from down in the dungeon room.

No answer.

"We need to leave," I say.

"The door is locked on the inside," across the bunk sister says.

"I know where the key is," I say.

"Michael?" Pa says.

His steps make no time to grab the key from the drawer in Ma and Pa's room.

I am standing by the front door when Pa reaches the top of the stairs. "What the fuc—"

Across the bunk sister uses her mighty strength to bang Pa with the bar. Pa loses his balance, and the sound of him tumbling down the stairs is like when I would lie listening to rain pitter patter on the roof and thunder would boom from above. That is a comforting sound. Now and then.

"C'mon," I say, holding my arm for across the bunk sister to grab. She does, and we run to Ma and Pa's room. I grab the same three keys from before. I find the correct one, first try this time, and we run. Hand in hand, we run and yell the loudest we ever have. Safety bars clank on the cement road behind us.

A woman comes running from her house. She looks horrified. I haven't seen myself in a very long time, and I probably look the same as across the bunk sister.

Very tired and very hungry.

"Help. I still have two more sisters and two brothers. Pa is in the dungeon room and Michael is sleeping at the top of the stairs," I say.

The woman hugs me as other neighbors rush outside to comfort the girls.

We did it. For the first time, I feel what Michael was talking about.

Hope. Hope for what comes next for us.

Because we did it.

We escaped.

We are finally free.

For the kids being held back by their own families.

The Cyst

"Looks like a cyst to me, son," the doctor said.

This was the third dermatologist I had been to, and they all told me the same thing. The bulging red, enflamed, painful growth on my neck was a cyst. They all prescribed me antibiotics to take the infection down. I swallowed the full dose for the past two months, and the growth sitting next to my jugular vein had amassed to a golf ball size.

"Okay, thank you, doc," I said and exited the room without any further consultation.

"I can prescribe you—"

The doctor's voice faded as I exited the corporate building combining doctors' offices, dentists' offices, and vaccination centers.

Back in my car, I welcomed the silence I knew wouldn't be there for long. I told these doctors that I couldn't move my head from left to right, I told these doctors my pain level was a ten out of ten, but what I left out was the voice growing in my head at the same rate the "cyst" was budding.

"Another doctor down and another failure for good ole Willy boy," the cyst said.

"Shut the fuck up," I said to the empty space of my vehicle.

The voice began, just as the bump did, as a minor faded nuisance I could live with but had grown to a clear, defined pain in the fucking ass.

"How can I shut the fuck up when I'm the one connected to the same brain you are? It's basically you arguing with yourself. Which if you ask me just makes you a crazy person. Especially if you wanna go do that in public. Woooeee. You'll look like a crackhead for sure."

Covering my ears only made the voice louder, and sleeping became impossible with constant goings on and never stopping.

"Maybe you need to see a brain doctor like a psychiatrist or psychotherapist for your troubles."

"I'm not a fucking psychopath."

"Whoa. Whoa. Whoa. I never said you are. And if you think people in therapy are crazy, then you are the one who needs a look in the mirror."

The mirror was exactly the place I never wanted to look again after this thing on my neck really took off.

Ignoring the voice was one thing, but the constant pain of scanning incoming traffic to turn onto Main Street that forced my shoulders to go with me at each intersection was not only embarrassing but horribly inconvenient. I felt like a robot whose head wasn't designed to swivel.

The cyst yapped the entire way back to my parents' house about anything and everything. "Hey, the Mets are doing horrible again. Who woulda thought." And "Did you hear that the president is running for a second term, what a joke of a guy." And "Can we watch that sitcom your mom always has on?" The perfect recipe for an unbearable existence.

"What did the doctor say, sweetheart?" Mom said when I walked through the door. She was sitting down watching her favorite sitcom. She had been so worried for the past couple months, commenting on how big it was getting, and how I should get a second and third opinion, and to make sure I'm taking the medication every day. The concern was expected and appreciated, but the cyst was the cause for my constant pounding headache, and I didn't need more noise.

"The same as the others. I need to lie down," I said and ran upstairs before she could speak another word.

When I graduated from high school two months ago, I thought it would be the beginning of my new life. Go to college to study sports journalism, have the time of my life living on campus a thousand miles away from my parents, and going to the same school as my best friend, but this cyst confined me to a summer of lying in my bed not able to sleep or turn on my side. What my life was now consisted of staring at the ceiling and waiting for things to improve as well as going to doctors' appointments for them to tell me there was nothing they could do besides RX intervention. One of the doctors, after pressing down on the cyst and me almost swinging my arms and smacking him in the face from the pain, suggested lancing the cyst, but it was impossible since it had not come to a head. Surgery was an option, but the doctor warned it was risky due to the location of the cyst.

"There's someone at your door. Hellloooo. Wake up, sleepy head."

Tuning out the voice was my only option, and I thought I'd gotten fairly good at it. I'd also gotten good at taking power naps. It was the only way to sleep since slumber wasn't coming at night.

"Uh, come in," I said, groggy and barely able to adjust to the overhead light that hadn't changed since the nap began.

"You doin' okay?" my dad asked and sat at the edge of my bed.

"Yeah. Yeah, totally," I said, not convincing even myself.

"It's just that your mom and I haven't seen you in a while, and you are not the kid we used to know."

That was an understatement. The summer months were the best times of my life. I was at parties, playing football with my rotating group of pals, a new summer fling each year. Now a party felt unmanageable, a football game on the beach would be impossible, and girls would take one look at me and retch their day's meals all over me.

"I'm good, Dad. Really, I am. Just nervous for college is all. I want to be ready."

"Well, that's kind of what I wanted to talk to you about," he began. "I know the thing on your neck is causing you pain and you can barely function, son. Your mom and I were thinking maybe you take the first semester off. Stay here and get that thing—"

"No," I said. The harshness caused Dad to jump back and stroke his white Fu Manchu goatee. "I just mean I don't wanna fall behind on my work and watch my best friend start without me."

"The work will always be there, and you can do it at your own pace and—"

"Dad, I said no."

"Wow, being disrespectful to the man who brought you into this world is a new low for you. Look how hurt and sad he looks," the cyst said.

"I'm looking out for your best interest," Dad continued. "Nonstop classes and back and forth between your dorm and any extracurricular activities you see yourself wanting to do will be shattered by constant pain."

"He's right, ya know. Why not just stay here for the fall, and we can hang out and count the spots of chili your parents never noticed when you splattered it onto the ceiling a month ago. What a ripping good time, don't ya think so, son."

The voice needed to stop. My dad was waiting for a response, anything from me. And what made the situation worse was Mom walking into my room and standing at the foot of my bed with her arms crossed. It was becoming less of a choice and more of a mandatory option.

"Honey, we just want what's best for you. Take some time to get your health situated and then college will be there. It's not going anywhere," Mom said.

"It's not gonna grow feet and walk away. She's right, it isn't," the cyst said, followed by a cackling, maniacal laughter. "You should stay, and we can have slumber parties every night, doesn't that just sound ravishing?"

"This is your choice. It absolutely is, but we are doing this out of love and strong suggestion," Dad said. "Just the fall semester, then in the winter you can hop on the plane, and we will see you on holidays."

"We're so proud of you," Mom said. "I really hope you know that. And we really know you will do well in your field of study."

"Sports journalism. The most laughable major is school history," the cyst said. "Why, so you can sit around all day drinking beer and watching grown men hit each other? That's what you want to report on? Something you already do that chases every woman you loved away. Because nobody wants to sleep with a useless, nobody, lazy, rotting piece of shit."

"Shut the fuck up." The words came out louder and clearer than any words I had ever spoken. It was directed at the cyst in my head, but locking eye contact with my mom in a quiet room was enough to well tears into her eyes.

"No, that wasn't—"

But it was too late; she was out of the room.

"As long as you live under this roof, you are under my rules. And respect is my biggest one," Dad said. "Especially to your mother. Now you have no choice. You already sit in this room all day, and now you will until I say you can go to school. I'm calling the registrar's office right now and letting them know not to expect you for a while. I don't know what happened to my kind son, but please bring him back to apologize to your mom."

He was out of the room with a sharp slam of the door for good measure.

"Phew, what a turn of events in so little time," the cyst said. I plugged my fingers in my ears. No matter how much it hurt, I turned on my side, but the talking continued. "Hey, maybe this is best for you. You were going to party your parents' money away anyhow. I mean—"

I got up and went into the bathroom adjacent to my room. Stopping to look in the mirror before opening it to access the medicine cabinet behind, I assessed the cyst. It was ugly, a deep red with purple veins intersecting throughout, bulging and growing to baseball size approaching my chin. Nothing was solving this problem, so I would solve it myself.

Inside the cabinet were orange pill bottles, some for me, some for Mom, some for Dad. But on the bottom shelf was a small razor blade rusted in black and sharp enough to scrape the leftover bathroom activities' gunk off the countertop.

"You really think that's a good idea?" the cyst said. "What do you think will happen when you cut me open?"

"You'll be gone forever."

"And so will you, stupid boy."

"At this point I don't really fucking care."

I held the razor blade between two fingers and used the mirror to make sure I was in the right spot. The pain I had felt each time I twisted my neck was nothing compared to dragging the blade across the bulbous growth. Sensors of pain were sent into the base of my skull and down my spine to my toes. Tears dripped from my ducts, but I continued all the same. My head buzzed and my vision was faltering.

Blood dripped onto my shoulders and the white tiles on the floor. I hadn't thought through the process of keeping the area clean. All I could think about was ridding my head of this thing.

Wooziness lifted the heaviness from my head, and I needed to catch my balance so as not to smack my head on the porcelain toilet. As the blade made a clean cut from one side of the ball to the other, green pus joined the exit party, and I tilted back, having a seat on the toilet. The noise travelled through the floor, and two sets of footsteps were growing closer.

"You fucking idiot. You are gonna get us killed," the cyst said. "You need me. I am the one who has helped you through this process. And you repay me by killing me. What kind of fucking friend does that to someone who—"

The time from sitting upright on the toilet to the floor was seconds, and my parents' feet were at my eye level as the voice inside faded and my mom's and dad's grew.

"Oh my god, call 911," Dad said.

"Stay with me," Mom said, phone pressed to her ear. Her brown and white curls were the last I saw before everything went black.

***

"Hey, buddy. Welcome back," a voice said before I could see anything. I hadn't gotten rid of it. Cutting the cyst out did not cure my head from the thing inside. Until I opened my eyes and a woman in a white coat, hazel eyes, and blonde hair stood over me. "There you are. Your parents have been super worried about you, but I told them I would take care of you."

"Oh my god, you're back. I was so, so worried," Mom said, hugging my torso.

"Why would you do something so stupid," my dad said in his warm welcome back to the living.

A new activity months in the making was I could turn my head from side to side, at least enough that the large bandage taped to the left side of my neck would allow.

"Sorry," I said with as much as my voice could muster through what felt like a collection of nails in my esophagus.

"It should take about three months to fully heal," the doctor said. "While there will be a noticeable scar, I'm sure that's something you wouldn't mind showing off."

A smile creased on my lips, and through the IV in my arm and another wire on my finger, I sat up in the hospital bed feeling better than I had felt since the cyst began growing.

"Mom," I said. Her hand touched mine. "I love you. You did nothing wrong."

She nodded in response, and that was enough for me to know all was forgiven. My dad would be tougher to forgive me, not for inadvertently yelling at my mom but for performing surgery on myself.

A few hours later, I was released from the hospital, and we sat at the kitchen table for a family dinner. It was an activity we hadn't done in years, mostly from my selfishness of getting older, not wanting to be seen as a loser who ate supper with his parents. But now I would do it until I left for school next semester.

"Thank you both. Really," I said before hugging each of them and returning to my room.

The posters of supermodels came down, and my sports heroes went up. Porn magazines under my bed went into the trash, and journalism books took up my nightstand. Things would be different, and I wouldn't let my parents down while I was away.

As I opened to the first page of the textbook I found online, a voice in my head spoke to me; it said—

For those with relentless acne struggles, you are seen.

A Conversation with Myself

My shower is a prison.

A twenty- to thirty-minute activity enclosed by tiled walls and a flimsy curtain. A time forcing you to observe your own body. The most vulnerable parts of you on display for you to see.

When I peer down, I see my hair follicles working overtime to push the disgusting body fur back through my pores. I had disposed of those only one day ago. This can't be an everyday occurrence. Shaving. Shaving extends my shower sentence from thirty minutes to over an hour.

At least my arms are clear, and the winter months help with clothing requirements for the single-digit temperatures outside. Jeans, three shirts, a big fluffy coat, and a hat and gloves. A look of nondescript. Nobody knows who I am, and that's the way I like it.

When I towel off and lotion up, I step three feet into the worst invention created by man. And you know a man created a mirror. Who else wants to stare into their own reflection and study how good they look for an eternity?

Not me.

Not me at all.

My long hair is my shield. I protect my head hat at any cost. It will sit at my shoulders and beyond forever.

If the bumps opening to hairs on my stomach and chest and legs and on my broad shoulders isn't enough for a mental break, the cheeks, chin, and upper lip are the devil.

I stare down my enemy. The muscle I stack on from my infrequent weightlifting sessions. The red splotches of acne dotting my epidermis. My five o'clock shadow. All shout out in unison. They call out, bouncing around inside my head.

"Change."

That word isn't in my head. It comes from in front of me.

Behind the mirror and wall is Gloria. Beautiful Gloria. She is in her slumber and can't make out a sound other than her light breathing and soft murmurs.

What can the word mean? Change what? Clothes? My mirror? My life?

"Change."

The word again.

This time I pay mind to myself. I am saying it. My mouth is moving beyond my control.

"It is time to make a change."

My mouth is closed. What is happening?

"Hello?" I say. Normal.

"Change."

"Stop saying that," I say.

Then there is a change. My hair grows in volumes. A black damp mess to a princess-esque curled fascination. My teenage—those years long gone—raging hormone, pimpled face clears to a clean and pretty one. Jaw line shrinks. Brows grow in definition. Lips curl to cupid's bow perfection. The birthmark under my right eye—the size of a ballpoint pen—remains. My breasts grow to a C. My torso shapes to an hourglass. My normally short legs grow to model status.

I feel the tears welling, and one escapes down my perfect cheekbone.

I make a mistake. I look down. My old body. Hairs are poking. The tears flow now. Uncontrollable.

Back at the mirror.

"Change is good," the lady says.

"Not for me," I say.

"Then suffer in your own wake," the lady says.

She's the one who changes. Her pale skin turns to a chalky gray. Her dreamy blue eyes extend into black, eliminating the white scleras. White teeth are now yellowed shards lining her mouth. It isn't a "she" any longer. It is a thing.

The thing reaches for me. Its lanky fingers leave the confines of the mirror and extend inches from my neck. It grasps the tendrils of my throat and squeezes.

I can feel it all. The cold, dead palm pressuring my larynx. The dirty fingernails pressing their hurt into my cervical vertebrae. My breath fleeting. My eyes blur. My screams are unheard.

I think fast. I kick the cabinet, the one under the sink. I kick and kick and kick until—

"Ben, what are you doing?" Gloria's beautiful voice. Gloria's beautiful face looking down upon my naked body.

"I-I-I—" Breathing is not an easy accomplishment. Also, I'm not sure how to answer the question presented.

"Are you okay?" Gloria says, her face switching from fright to one of concern.

"I-I'm okay. Just fell." I stand and embrace her. She seems surprised but squeezes me tight, just as she forever has.

The woman's reflection has disappeared.

And hopefully not forever.

***

Childhood trauma is what I hear the most.

Something happened when you were five years old that makes you the way you are.

If I had a traumatic event when I was young, I certainly don't recall it.

My parents supported me "one million percent. In anything you do," they would say.

I wanted to be an artist at the age of six years old. Mom bought me a sixty-four pack of crayons and a pad filled with blank pages, allowing my imagination to run wild. I would sit cross-legged on my bed for hours and create what filled my mind. Tigers, lions, bears, houses, street signs, Mom, Dad, younger sister, myself.

When I was doodling up a self-portrait, I drew legs with pants, a torso and arms with a sweater, an oval head, but when it came to my own face, it remained blank. I made so many attempts at drawing myself. I would cut a ninety-degree angle for the nose, erase it. Almond eyes, erase it. My small lips, erase it. I eventually just left a single dot. The birthmark was all I saw when looking at myself in the devastating reflection.

I open the side table drawer next to my bed. I pull out three pads full of my scribblings. Many more are strewn about the home. I held on to the ones from the very first line to the immaculate artistry of yesterday. It is the story of my life. Every day for thirty years. I live my day out, go home, collect my colored pencils, and create what I am feeling on that particular day.

I flip past the art of days past. For today it is the mirror monster. And it will be my final drawing.

I start with the vertical rectangular-looking glass. At the top are gold trim flowers adding design to the reflection deathtrap. In the forefront I scribble my oval head, straight hair extending to mid-back, and shoulder to complete the outline.

When I try to draw the woman I saw, I am restricted. My hand won't extend to the paper. Not by my own doing, but by some force refusing to be placed on paper. Gloria has gone off to work, so if any otherworldly events occur, I am on my own.

I typically work afternoons, but I called an hour ago—seconds after Gloria left—and quit. I don't need it any longer, and they won't miss me. My boss took it as a joke and said, "Okay, see you in a few hours."

My parents are six feet under, and my sister is with her drug-pushing boyfriend three states over. Aunts and uncles are sprinkled all over the country and haven't spoken a word or text to me in ages. The group of guys I was close to in high school has moved away, and our only communication is a Facebook message every couple of months. My one and only friend is Gloria. She will miss me. We met when I quite literally ran into her at a coffee shop. She was covered in chai latte and vanilla frosting. The time between my help cleaning the mess and our first kiss was hours apart. Our love is electric, and she is all I need. But, once my final drawing is complete, she will find someone new who can be who she needs in a relationship. Not somebody with loads of baggage who refuses to speak on it.

I try again.

A hand holds my wrist back. The same gray hand has come through the wall to confine my movements. I press closer as I feel the grip loosening. I can complete this. I will complete this. The grip breaks and when the pencil hits the paper, the tip snaps.

"Just leave me alone," I shout to the empty walls.

This is all in my head. There is nothing living in my mirror. I am just having an internal crisis prior to committing an act looked down upon by many.

It's my life and I can do anything I damn well please with it. I didn't ask to be born. I didn't ask for this brain. I just want to live a normal life and be a normal person. But society won't allow that. Society is built on normalcy. If a majority of persons are a certain way, do certain things, then all should follow suit. What kind of backwards place was I driven into? What life is this? What is this life?

"Fuck it."

I throw my pad to the floor, Gloria's dress flowing behind me as I scoot to the kitchen. I pull a knife from the block. A long serrated blade, good for cutting bread. And wrists.

Three years old. I was three years old when I was standing in the middle of a Walmart, stomping my feet and crying incessantly all because my parents refused to buy me the clothing I wanted. They told me it wasn't what I supposed to be wearing. They aren't to blame. They didn't know any better. It was what they were taught. There was a non-stop pressure to not make your son look like a faggot. Such words from the eighties and nineties used in normal rotation by bigoted assholes pushing their religious views on everybody in earshot. Religion, one of preaching kindness and solidarity with all, except…

What a life. What a fucking life I don't want to be a part of any longer.

I stand with the knife in my right hand pressed to my left wrist.

"Where are you? Where the fuck are you?" The jagged teeth press into my skin. Blood has already begun to flow. Dots of red spot the cold white tiles my feet stand upon.

"C'mon. Stop me. Why aren't you stopping me?" Tears return. Now with sucking sobs. I am an ugly crier. My mouth agape. Water staining the stubble on my cheeks. "Wh-why. Please stop me from doing this. I don't want to. I just want to live life on my terms. My own fucking life the way I want. Free of ridicule. Free of hate. Pl-ple—"

I slide down the wall opposite my reflection. The knife clangs to the tile surface. There is a deep slash of crimson gurgling out of my limp arm. That is not how I imagined it would happen. It happens differently when you see it on TV shows and movies.

Lightheadedness has kicked in. That was expected. Next will be death.

I'm sorry, Gloria.

I'm sorry for not saying goodbye.

And I'm sorry for getting blood on your favorite Michael Kors dress.

***

My angel.
My savior.
My Gloria.

She is looking down upon me again. Tears in her eyes. This time I lay in a hospital bed. In an ugly nightgown with a draft I can feel blowing up my ass.

"I love you." Gloria has said those words one hundred, one thousand times since I woke and over the course of our seven-year relationship.

"I believe you," I say, one hundred, one thousand times in return.

I lift my left arm, and the heavy bandages from mid-forearm to middle knuckles is not fun. It won't be fun for the next four weeks when it can be taken off. Though it does need to be re-bandaged twice a day. Gloria has already volunteered for that duty.

Hours later, we are back in our home. My blood is stained to the bathroom floor. I enter, but a hand pulls me back into the hall. Gloria. A terrified, somber look plasters her face.

"I'm just going to use the bathroom," I say.

"Why wouldn't you talk to me? I'm not mad or anything like that. I just wa—just want you to know you can talk to me about anything."

I sigh. Not in a way of showing I'm tired of hearing that. She says that to me each and every day. And she asks "what's wrong" along with it.

"It's nothing," I say now and again for the one hundredth, one thousandth time.

Gloria scans the bathroom. The towel and its rack broken; the knife still next to the bathmat. "It is not nothing."

"I know. But that's my safety phrase. A phrase that comforts you. It is a lie. There is so much wrong. And I plan on telling you everything, but I need to have a conversation with myself first," I say.

Gloria nods and plants a wet, cold kiss on my cracked, disgusting lips. The one hundredth, one thousandth kiss that feels different this time. Not quite right just yet, but different. A good different.

I enter my near-death layer and close the door.

I stare into the mirror. My own worst enemy.

"Hello, Jennifer. It's nice to finally meet you."

For those struggling with identity.

The Grambler

The following transcript is recovered
cell phone footage found after the flood of 2016.

Chase Sandusky: Do you really need to record this whole adventure?

Katelyn Hill: Yes! If we find The Grambler, we can get it on video, then send it to news stations, then we can ask for tons of money for them to show it.

Chase: I don't think that's how that works, sweetheart.

Katelyn: Well, then we can put it on YouTube, and we can become famous, and they'll make a movie about us starring Johnny Depp—since people always say you look like a young Johnny Depp.

Chase: Nobody has ever said that.

Katelyn: Well, I think so. Shouldn't that be enough? Anyway, Emma Watson can play me because…just because I like Emma Watson.

Chase: With the world the way it is, that is, believe it or not, the more likely thing to happen. Movie studios are desperate for original content.

Katelyn: Hey, don't forget your backpack, Chase.

Chase: We're only planning on being down there for a couple hours. I don't see the need to carry around all this stuff.

Katelyn: If we somehow get stuck down there, then you'll be thanking me that you have food. And more importantly, I don't have to hear you whine about how hungry you are, like you always do.

Chase: That is not true.

Katelyn: On our first date you complained to the poor waitress because you had to wait thirty minutes for your food to get there.

Chase: Plus, thirty minutes waiting for a table.

Katelyn: Well, regardless, you have energy bars and those snack packs of vegetables that you like.

Chase: Thanks.

Katelyn: Ready to head out?

Chase: I guess.

Katelyn: It won't be that bad, trust me.

Chase: But do we really need to do this at one in the morning?

Katelyn: I have explained this to you so many times. The Grambler only comes out when it's dark and everyone is sleeping. Plus, our parents would murder us if they found out our plans.

Chase: You mean *your* plans. I'm just doing this because I was dragged into it. By you.

Katelyn: Whatever. I'm not forcing you to do anything. I just thought it'd be a fun couple adventure.

Chase: I'm here, Katelyn. I could still be at my house playing *Call of Duty*, but I'm here and ready to go. I also know you would go without me, and I can't let you go down there on your own.

Katelyn: And I appreciate that more than you know.

Chase: It's just…

Katelyn: What?

Chase: It's just strange that people have only seen this Grambler thing in the shadows. From what you told me, nobody has ever gotten a good look at it.

Katelyn: If you do a Google search, there are so many images. It's seven feet tall, it wears a top hat, and is missing skin.

Chase: And you really believe that?

Katelyn: Of course. There's even a video of it walking through the woods.

Chase: There's also a video of Bigfoot in the woods. That doesn't mean it's not some guy in a costume.

Katelyn: And how many seven-foot people do you know?

Chase: None, but they exist.

Katelyn: So, you admit The Grambler could exist.

Chase: Look, I'm skeptical about most things I see on the internet. I'm sorry if this makes you upset, but I think this is a waste of time.

Katelyn: Then don't come. I'll do this on my own. Goodbye.

Chase: Don't be that way.

Katelyn: I'm not forcing you, but I would really like you by my side for this.

Chase: Every step of the way. Plus, I'm not going to explain to your mother how you were eaten by a fictional monster.

Katelyn: The Grambler doesn't eat people, Chase.

Chase: Either way. With her divorce, losing her daughter would devastate her. And I know I haven't known her very long, but I like her.

Katelyn: That means so much to me. Thank you. Now let's go find this thing.

***

Chase: We really need to climb down there? We can't just summon the monster up here?

Katelyn: I thought I was the female in the relationship.

Chase: It's not about that.

Katelyn: What's it about then?

Chase: It's about not catching a disease or being mauled by wild animals.

Katelyn: You know there aren't really alligators down there, right?

Chase: What about…

Katelyn: Or evil clowns. You need to watch less movies.

Chase: And you need to read less conspiracies on the internet.

Katelyn: Okay, fine. Let's make a bet. If the The Grambler is down there, you owe me one hundred dollars.

Chase: Have you forgotten I work part-time at Frank's Pizzeria prepping food? I know Frank's has been in town for years, but they don't pay their employees well. I barely make fifty dollars a week.

Katelyn: Fine. Fifty dollars for me if it's down there.

Chase: And if there's no sign of this thing?

Katelyn: That's not fair because we might just not come across it while we're down there.

Chase: Katelyn.

Katelyn: Okay, fine. Fifty dollars if we don't see it.

Chase: Shake on it.

Chase: Or a kiss works too.

Katelyn: Help me with this cover.

Chase: It might help if you put the phone down.

Chase: Shit, these things are heavy.

Katelyn: No kidding. C'mon. Let's drop in. You first.

Chase: Ugh, it stinks.

Katelyn: This is where everybody's poop goes. Obviously it stinks.

Chase: When you drop down, stay on the side since the middle is water and I'm not sure how deep…Katelyn!

Katelyn: I slipped off that stupid cement side. But, to answer your curiosity, the water comes up to my waist. More importantly, my phone is safe. Grab the flashlight out of your backpack and I'll use the one on my phone. I need it for good footage anyway.

Chase: Shouldn't we put the cover back on in case a car drives by?

Katelyn: Do you wanna lift that thing again when we need to get out of here?

Katelyn: I didn't think so.

Chase: Isn't your new, fancy phone waterproof, anyway?

Katelyn: Getting water on it is the last thing I'm worried about.

Chase: So, is there a particular direction we should be going?

Katelyn: This way.

Chase: And you're sure about that how?

Katelyn: Because in my research, I found a local article saying there was a sighting a few streets that way.

Chase: Okay. It's easier if you come up here. Give me your hand and I'll pull you up.

Katelyn: I'm fine in the water.

Chase: That is disgusting. There is no way I'm kissing you again until you take fifteen showers.

Katelyn: Oh hush. You don't think I know what I'm walking around in? Besides, The Grambler lives in the water passages.

Chase: And that's why I am perfectly content up here.

Katelyn: And what happens when we come to a place where there's no more safety wall to stand on?

Chase: I'd rather not think about that right now.

Katelyn: Good. Let's focus on finding our new friend.

Chase: I don't get how you're so comfortable with this.

Katelyn: I find it interesting. Just like you find video games and movies interesting.

Chase: Yes, because those don't require you to walk through freaking sewers.

Katelyn: All you have done since we started this is complain and complain. You know the way out.

Chase: I'm sorry. Tell me more about this gambler then.

Katelyn: Grambler. According to the legend, he started as a normal guy who worked in a factory back in the 30s.

Chase: The 1930s?

Katelyn: Yes, Chase. Now listen. He never stayed in one place for very long. They think it's because he had a gambling addiction. He would make lots of money from his job—at least it was a lot of money back then—then he would gamble it away, not be able to afford his house, and move to a different state or city to start again.

Chase: Sounds like my dad.

Katelyn: The article I read said he lived here the longest.

Chase: Stratford or Connecticut?

Katelyn: Stratford. He was becoming super successful with his gambling and his job.

Chase: I'm guessing he didn't live happily ever after.

Katelyn: One night a burglar broke into his home after it got out that he became super wealthy fairly quick. He found the masked thief going through his stash, and the startled burglar shot him once in the chest. Scared of being taken in for murder instead of a little theft, the burglar took off. The Grambler wasn't married and had abandoned his family. So, he lay there on the floor, unable to move, for two days until a nosy neighbor looked through his window and saw him dead.

Katelyn: And when the neighbor got inside to help, all of the money and jewels were gone.

Chase: The neighbor could have just lied, or the burglar could have come back and finished the job.

Katelyn: The police did a search of the neighbor's home, and the burglar was never found. Nothing was ever found.

Chase: Then what happened to it?

Katelyn: They say he somehow moved his things from his bedroom down to the sewer so it would always be safe. Now his ghost wanders underground, stopping anybody who tries to steal from him again.

Katelyn: Why are you laughing?

Chase: I'm sorry, but that sounds like something from a kid's show. He wanders the sewers protecting his missing money from a bunch of years ago. I don't buy it.

Katelyn: Then what is that?

Chase: What, that glowing? Probably just a streetlight shining through a drain.

Katelyn: I don't think so.

Chase: It's…no.

Katelyn: Yes. You better get your fifty dollars ready.

Chase: That doesn't mean anything. Somebody probably put this down here to scare people like you.

Katelyn: What are you doing?

Chase: Jumping into the water so I can get a better look.

Katelyn: Don't touch it.

Chase: Why not? I thought you weren't afraid.

Katelyn: I never said that. I said I was interested. And I've been interested enough. Let's go.

Chase: No. I think we should take some.

Katelyn: Chase. Do not touch that. Chase!

Chase: What? I'm just taking one coin. We need to prove we saw this. Am I right?

Katelyn: No. You need to put that back and we need to leave.

Chase: We can leave. But finders keepers.

Katelyn: I really don't think you should have done that.

Chase: Relax. Nothing is gonna happen. Let's go.

Katelyn: You don't know that.

Chase: I know that you dragged me out here and I find something I see as interesting and suddenly, I'm the bad person.

Katelyn: You don't understand. People have taken from him before and were never seen again. Including those burglars.

Chase: It's just a fairy tale. You need to learn that the internet is filled with false information just to scare people.

Katelyn: But these are real…wait, is the water getting higher?

Chase: It might be. But we could just be walking through a dip in the floor.

Katelyn: No, Chase. The floor hasn't changed. I walked this same path on the way here. It was always at my waist. Now it's almost at my neck.

Chase: Look, don't panic. We don't have too much farther to go.

Katelyn: No. It's the gold coin. You need to put it back.

Chase: I played along with your games the whole time, now you're just getting annoying.

Katelyn: Chase. You need to believe me.

Chase: You dragged me down here.

Katelyn: Yes. And now I regret it. I'm sorry, but please put it back.

Chase: Tread the water. Kate!

Katelyn: I…don't…know…how…to…

Chase: I do. I'll pull you along. Don't let go of my hand.

Katelyn: Hurry. The water's rising faster.

Chase: It would help if you put the phone away.

Katelyn: No. My mom would kill me.

Chase: Well, I'm going as fast as—

Katelyn: Something grabbed my leg.

Chase: It's just your imagination. We're almost back to the sewer hole.

Katelyn: It just grabbed me again. Chase, I don't like this. I'm scared.

Chase: C'mon, we can make—

Katelyn: Chase!

Chase: We need to move now.

Katelyn: What happened?

Chase: I was pulled under.

Katelyn: By what?

Chase: I don't know, and I don't want to find out.

Katelyn: Ch-ch-ch-ase.

Chase: What?

Katelyn: There's a bone floating next to you.

Chase: Oh fuck.

Katelyn: Go faster.

Chase: I fucking can't.

Katelyn: Chase. A skull. There's a human skull. And it's moving.

Chase: It's just the water moving it.

Katelyn: No, you don't get—

Chase: Kate!

Katelyn: It pulled me…

Chase: What the fuck is that thing?

Unknown male voice: Stealing is for the weak. Return my coin at once.

Katelyn: Give him his coin back, Chase.

Chase: No, I see the exit.

Unknown male voice: Stupid teenagers. You have tried before and failed. Now I have more to add to my bone collection. Young bones make me feel like I did back in the day. They make me feel alive.

Katelyn: Chase. You are such a bonehead.

Chase: I can make it.

Katelyn: The exit isn't an option anymore.

Joe Baldwin

Chase: I'm here. Give me—

Katelyn: It's got my leg. Help.

Chase: You got yourself into this mess.

Katelyn: Please don't leave me. Please, Chase, I love—

For Mom, who started my love for urban legends.

The Weatherman

Jordan Laymon- I can't believe you get paid to lie.

Becky Groton- So ridiculous.

Nathan Bachman- 6 inches predicted and got a dusting. What a joke!

Larry Oscar- You shouldn't have a job!

I know I shouldn't read the comments under my videos, but there is something about human curiosity that draws one in. Hate comments are low in comparison to the internet community I have built up over the years. I have friends that I talk to in my DMs that I only know through Facebook. They are what I look forward to when I open my eyes each morning.

But one bad comment equals about a hundred good ones. Somebody telling you to quit your job or that you should be fired just climbs into your gut and twists it around like a washing machine. There is no good outcome responding to the internet trolls, so I remain quiet and continue pushing forward.

Meteorology is a tough profession. It is taking a projection from a computer model, multiple computer models, and using the ever-changing data to make an estimated guess at the weather for a small portion of the world. The ones saying the nasty things in the chat wouldn't last a week doing this job. But social media is just that, people with no experience screaming and whining about things they don't know a word about.

They graduated from Facebook University with a degree in shit-talking. They are nobodies sitting in their momma's basement who think they know everything while I am making a ton of money and furthering my life.

Social media is bad, but nothing compares to the winter months. As a kid I prayed each night, shivering in my bed, that mountains of snow would be on the ground in the morning. It didn't happen often, but when it did come, I was away from the kids at school and buried deep in the white powdery goodness.

Snow still fascinates me, and I look forward to it each year, but that is when predictions are the toughest and the hatred is the roughest. Not only do the internet trolls tear me down, but my boss might be worse. Mr. Terry counts on my prediction to be accurate or at least in the same ballpark. He cares about ratings, and that is something that doesn't concern me. I care about spreading the word about the weather. Seeing kids' smiling faces when I visit schools and teach them about climate, fronts, and how snow forms in the clouds brings me the greatest joy I have ever known.

"Billy. In my office now," Mr. Terry says.

I follow him inside his stuffy office, stuffy even in February. I sit across from him, and I know what this is concerning.

"Way off, Billy. Way off," Mr. Terry says.

"I know. The European model is never the closer amount."

"Never?"

"Rarely. It's rare."

"So rare that my ratings plummeted during your weather report?" Mr. Terry says with his bushy eyebrows in a state of question, but his brown eyes showing he knows the answer to the inquiry.

"I'm sorry. But I don't get why people are upset. No snow is what they should be rooting for. No shoveling. No sliding around on the roads."

"Because people depend on certain things. In anticipation, events are cancelled, schools are closed, money is lost, then poof, a miracle, no snow whatsoever."

I rub my temples to attempt to perform a miracle on my pounding migraine. "It won't happen again," I say.

"That's what you said the other times we held this same discussion." Mr. Terry rests his arms on his desk, and his facial features soften. "Look, I know your job is tough and you don't have a crystal ball, but ratings mean money for you, for me, for Tim the sports guy. You get me?"

I nod.

"Good, because if a mishap like this happens again. You're going to leave me no choice."

I hide the look of shock behind my hands.

I get up and walk out into the studio without a response. Cries of "that's not fair" and "you do my job for a day" would further damage the already tainted relationship with Mr. Terry.

I prepare my seven-day forecast to present to the citizens of Connecticut, then will hop on my social media for a discussion I am not looking forward to. A snow system is set to hit the area on the sixth day. It's shaping to be a large storm. The European model is showing fifteen inches. The American is predicting seven inches. A wide gap not fair for any meteorologist.

It's the storm of the century for me.

If I get this one wrong, it's my head.

***

The live Channel 8 segment went well. I didn't stutter or choke up when I told the audience that a big storm was brewing for the future. I didn't give any amounts, nor did I on my social media live video chat. There were the typical moans and groans of a big storm, but a majority remained cordial throughout.

I shrug my jacket on. A warm coat is every weatherperson's must have. On snow days I step outside the studio to shoot a video to show and measure the amounts piling up. It can take some hours to perfect the videos, and my fur hooded warmth has been a life saver.

I say my goodbyes and head up Whalley Avenue. I rent an apartment that is a ten-minute walk from the studio. I chose a place just up the street so I can take the opportunity each day to experience what many are going to walk out into. If I climbed into a warm vehicle and drove to the warm studio, I wouldn't be able to truly connect with my viewers.

Many patrons are settling in for a beer at the local bars, heading to and from classes at the school up the road, or just taking in the cold weather. The current temperature is ten degrees Fahrenheit, and it feels like my fingers are going to freeze to my phone.

I'm back to reading the comments under the video I posted this morning. Breath pluming from my mouth, informing everyone to bundle up because it's going to be a cold week.

Becky Groton- Are you sure it won't be 60 and sunny? Lmao

Brandon Better- I'll bring my shorts just in case.

Mildred Gates- Thanks for the info. I can always trust you, Billy.

I decide I've had enough internet for the walk home. Besides, I enjoy the sights and sounds of Godard Park. The frost on the trees shimmers. The tourists—mostly here for Yale—take photos.

But getting solicited by the homeless sleeping on the ground in their dirty sleeping bags and lice-infested hair, surrounded by empty liquor bottles purchased courtesy of the handouts from foolish strangers, is an avoidance I am happy with.

"Hey," an unkempt man says from his seat on the ground, an empty bench beside him.

"Sorry, no cash on me today," I say. I've given change to him before and I'm not a charity. I worked my way through school, at the news station, and worked my ass off so I didn't end up where this man is living.

"I take credit cards now," he says. "Look." He flips around to his hands and knees; his ass crack is nearly halfway out.

I shield the view with my hands. "That's a quick way to hypothermia," I say.

"Nah. I woulda gotten that years ago if that's the case."

I nod. "Well, you stay warm." A type of tip he doesn't want but one he can put to good use.

As I begin to walk on, he says, "You that weather guy I see on the news?"

I stop. I don't like talking with anyone about my occupation. As much as I enjoy the chatter about the weather, when I'm off the clock, I turn to a horror book as opposed to watching tornado documentaries. But I know this guy, so I engage. "I in fact am."

"No shoot. I knew I'd recognized you. You on one of the TVs they have on in the bars."

"Thanks for watching," I say, bored with his banter. My hands are beginning to hurt. I'm going to get hypothermia if I don't move along.

"Oh, yes, sir. You say days ago we g'tting' lots a snow. Then nothin'," the bearded man says.

Suddenly my hands warm, as does my wind whipped face. "Not an easy job. Predicting the weather."

"Wish you had one of them time machines, go to the future, then come back and say the right amount."

"That would be the dream scenario," I say, finished with politeness. "Okay, thanks for the talk. I gotta get home now."

"I can do that for you, ya know?" he says, and for some reason I'm intrigued.

"What can you do?"

"Make all the things that come out your mouth factual statements."

I shake my head. "Thanks for the offer, but I'll have to pass."

"It's the truth."

"Again. Th—"

Before I can move, his hands are clasped to my shoulders, and a twinge of pain radiates from my neck down to the tips of my toes. "What are y—"

Words are difficult to come by and my head spins. Godard Park has become a blurred mess of greens and whites. I am staring into the bloodshot eyes of the homeless man. The white hairs in his long beard dance around, and his tattered clothes drop from his body. A naked man is holding me, and I can't release his grip from me.

Just as I gain the strength back into my arms to push him away, I feel myself falling. Falling through the cement walk, through the dirt and grime of the earth, through the crest of the planet, and into oblivion.

***

I feel like I've been hit by a truck. My torso is sore, like I'm getting ready to fight the roughest flu of my life. I try to sit up, but my arms won't lift, and my legs aren't of any help. My throat feels like it hasn't had a drop of water in weeks, and my spinning head further proves that point.

The sunshine through the window, especially during the winter, is not a great indicator. I do sit up this time and I am nearly knocked back to the mattress.

I reach for my phone. Seventeen missed calls. Twenty-three text messages. And no alarm beeping. It's 8:40 a.m. I don't even normally sleep that late on my days off. My 4 a.m. workday wake-up has trained my body to get up for that time each morning.

I steady my feet, throw on my button down, slacks, dress shoes, whip my receding hair into a neat swish, shrug my winter jacket on my shoulders, and I'm out the door by 8:50.

I quicken my pace through Godard Park. The homeless are missing, as are the normal out-of-towners that infest the park at this time of day.

I don't have time to think about what happened yesterday. No time to consider the possibilities of what could have knocked me out for fifteen hours straight. My job is already in hot water, and while I have never been late in my five years at Channel 8, tardiness is a great reason for Mr. Terry to fire me.

I'm inside just in time for the 9 a.m. broadcast, and Susie, the head anchor, is running through the top stories of the day. On a typical day, I know the stories from the three pre-rehearsals I watch as I prepare for my segment.

Mr. Terry is frantically waving me into his office. Is it stuffier than yesterday?

He closes the door gently, but I can feel his want to slam it to high hell. He sits, and I take the seat across from him. The principal's office twice in one week.

"Are you kidding me? I've been trying to call you all morning. I thought you were dead, for cripes' sake," he says through gritted teeth.

"Sorry, I don't know what happened. I—"

"I don't care about your lame excuses, just get out there. You're on in five."

The knot in my stomach returns. Five minutes is barely enough time to set up, nevertheless give a report. I have forgotten my seven-day forecast, other than the snowstorm.

Luckily, the first half of the broadcast is a teaser for the full forecast later in the hour. I stand in front of the green screen; the graphics are displayed on the screen in front of me.

The current temperature and the highs and lows for today flash in my eyes. I repeat what is written on the screen and tell the viewers I will return with the seven-day forecast.

I have ten minutes to study my forecast, the cycling map of flurries happening later this afternoon, and present it confidently to the viewers.

This job is a ton more than repeating what's in front of me. It takes brain power to pick out certain terms and phrases, especially during the live streams when viewers are asking questions.

Now, there are only the viewers who can't interact, which puts my mind at ease.

"And, now to Bill Simmons for the weather. How are things looking out there, Bill? Rumors of a storm?" Susie Graham says.

I freeze.

I don't remember anything about meteorology. The man in the park must have sucked my brain of all my knowledge.

"Yeah, Susie. Possibility for a big storm on the horizon."

"How many inches?"

She typically shuts her trap after she passes the anchor baton to me. I can feel sweat dripping off my pits, and a stain doesn't look good on TV.

"F-fifteen inches. At least what it looks like now."

"Wow. Might need to stay in the studio for a couple days."

"For sure. But, before we get there, a few flurries this afternoon that will amount to nothing. Looks cold and dry for the reminder of the week, then that storm beginning on Saturday morning and ending on Sunday morning."

I never give the duration of the storm, but the flashing red light and my brain fart result in diarrhea of the mouth.

"Back to you, Susie."

When Susie chats about a local woman's dog attack, I take a breather, and Mr. Terry comes charging toward me.

"A week in advance? There's no way fifteen inches is gonna happen."

Mr. Terry is a smart man. He knows business, but he doesn't know the weather. Bill Simmons knows the weather.

***

Saturday approaches fast, and I am glad to be at home to watch the snow fall. I pick up my phone and the hate comments from the keyboard warriors are worse than ever. My phone goes back inside my pocket not worried about any opinions when reality wins every time.

My walks to work have been quiet. No homeless men in the park. No crazy voodoo dreams. No being unconscious for long periods of time.

I often think back on that. I can't put the pieces together. I have a vivid recollection of every second up to the moment of my blackout. The conversation. Him grabbing my shoulders. The man's naked body dancing in front of me. It's like he unknowingly injected me with a drug. But the biggest question mark of the entire situation is how the hell I ended up back in my own bedroom.

The oddity during the week that made me and Mr. Terry over the moon was my perfect temperature gauging. Tuesday, I predicted a high of twenty degrees. The high was twenty degrees. I predicted a low of two. The low was two. And the flurries came down, not sticking anywhere in the state. I'm typically a few degrees off and am typically five to ten up or down, but to be right on the money earns me a glass of red wine on Saturday night.

*****

I fear I overslept again when I check my phone and it is blown up with phone calls and texts. When my sleepy brain snaps in place, I realize it's Sunday and I don't go to work.

I search through texts and Facebook comments, and they all have a similar message. The amount for the entire state came in at fifteen inches exactly. I jump on my bed in excitement, not caring if my downstairs neighbors are annoyed. I am keeping my job, and I will be hailed for an exact forecasted weather week.

Then the hate comments roll in saying I had a lucky week, and it will be back to normal next week.

When next week rolls around after a lazy celebratory Sunday, I give the people what they want.

I do my normal routine of early morning Facebook video standing in front of the piles of snow extracted from the news studio parking lot. I stand on the hardened pile for the human-to-pile ratio. I give no indication to the viewers, the other anchors, or Mr. Terry of my intentions.

This little gag may get me fired, but after a perfect week and Mr. Terry handing me a wine gift basket this morning for a job well done, I think it will be a laugh riot. If Mr. Terry thinks the ratings flew through the roof last week, wait until he hears about the weather for tomorrow.

I'm up, and I go through the normal motions of temperatures for the week, sure to leave out tomorrow for effect.

"As you might have noticed, I left out tomorrow's numbers. We just got a new report on the European model." I look nervously at my boss, who looks to be visibly shaking. With fear or rage, I can't tell. When I click the button to the next slide, I have my answer. "We have a warm front coming up from Florida. I expect the streets to be flooded with melting snow with highs reaching one hundred degrees by tomorrow afternoon."

Mr. Terry's normal pale complexion is beat red when my segment ends.

"Are you kidding me? Is this some kind of joke?"

"Think of the ratings," I say. Half mocking him, half throwing truth bombs.

"Fuc—" He collects himself. "Ratings are going to drop when the temperature is ninety degrees colder than their trusted weatherman says."

I do feel a tad of shame, but I plan on correcting myself on my live stream later this afternoon.

But that never happens. My boss's boss calls the studio ten minutes after that conversation and instructs Mr. Terry to fire me.

He does just that.

***

I am the type of person that, no matter the temperature on the outside, the inside of my place of residence is an icebox so I can drift off to sleep.

This morning, I am dripping from every pore. My bedsheet has left an imprint of my sleeping position. I'm a back sleeper.

"What the fu—"

I sit up and am dizzied for a moment, I'm guessing by the amount of water my body has lost. I catch my balance, approach the window, and my corneas are stung by the radiant sunlight. I have a momentary adjustment before my mouth drops open farther than it's ever been. The streets are impassable with three inches of water rushing down Imperial Street as if God had decided it was a good place for a stream. The mountains of snow the Department of Transportation had run out of room to place, blocking the view of drivers crossing dangerous intersections, are liquid.

I rush to the side table for my phone. I tap The Weather Channel app—unreliable, but Channel 8 is dead to me—the current temperature is 96 degrees. At nine in the morning.

I drop my phone to the floor and sit on the edge of my wet bed. What the fuck is happening?

The vibrating against the hardwood floor startles me. I pick it up and Mr. Terry is calling. I deny the call. He will want one of two things: to bring me back in and do the weather for the rest of eternity or sit in silence in awe of my weather wizardry. Either way, I don't want to hear his nasal tone.

I fear opening any social media app, but curiosity gets the best of me. Facebook is filled with part wonderment of how this could be happening. I am on the same side as that group. The other side is angry. They are angry because the drastic change in the weather will affect their immune system.

I close my phone, click on the TV. Channel 8 has my face above Susie's right shoulder, and underneath, it reads: *Wizard or phony?*

Not interested in what the banter is, I flip through the channels. Sports, soap operas, morning game shows, CNN. My face, the picture from my bio on the Channel 8 website, is on CNN. They are flashing through shots of a flooded New Haven while discussing the impact global warming is having on the earth.

The TV is off, my gray sweatsuit donned, and I am out the door. I can feel my equilibrium shift as the heat sucks me dry. But I need to not be recognized. With my face plastered on national news, somebody will recognize me, and I can only imagine what comes next.

***

Downtown is easy enough to maneuver but a bit tougher slopping through a rush of running waters. On the outskirts is Campaign Hope. They are a corporation that feeds, clothes, and sleeps the homeless. The man who did this to me has to be in here.

I walk inside and I instantly feel I am in the wrong place. Each picnic table style bench is filled with tired, haggard citizens who surely haven't gotten a wink of sleep in ages. Whatever their situation is that led them to this point in their lives, it doesn't matter. They should be able to live comfortably like the rest of the money-hogging Americans. I live comfortably in an apartment and haven't given a thought to the ones I pass each day, hoping to receive a penny or dime to add to a single cheeseburger. Now, with my financial future in jeopardy, I see myself sitting at the same tables with the lowest of the low in the eyes of the country.

My childhood was comfortable with two wealthy, loving parents who paid my way through private elementary, middle, high school, and college. Not everyone is so lucky to have an easy life.

There is a line formed around the buffet stand and workers are plopping bright yellow eggs onto white plates, then on to the next volunteer with bacon, and down the line.

A sign at the end reads: *Only one serving per person. No refills.*

It's like walking through a high school cafeteria where the students are all in their forties and fifties. Although when I see a kid who looks around eighteen, my heart drops. When you reach adulthood, they boot you from the foster homes with no path on where to go next.

I sit across from the kid who is sitting by his lonesome.

He looks up from his plate of breakfast. "The fuck you want?" he says.

"Just wondering if you know a guy. He's got—"

"I don't know nobody. Now fucking get lost."

I keep my composure calm. "If I could just—"

"Are you fucking deaf? Leave."

The entirety of the hall stops their chewing to look in our direction.

"The kid said to leave him be," a voice from behind says.

A baseball mitt hand on my shoulder.

I turn and see a man with a long dark beard, white hairs poking through.

"You," I say. It comes out in a whisper, unsure if he hears me.

"Let's talk outside," he says and walks off without giving me a chance to respond.

The surrounding neighborhood is one where someone like me doesn't belong.

"You're looking for me, huh?" he says.

"Yeah. Whatever you did to me, it wo—"

"I know. I told you I could help you. So, what's the big deal? You got what you wanted."

"How do you even know that I wanted that? I never said—"

"Let me tell you somethin'…" He places a hand on my shoulder, and I wince, thinking I'm going to be shot back into the alternate reality. "…some people have a dream where they kill their own mama. Some people have diseases, some people's bodies move without them movin' it. What I'm sayin' is, I don't know why people do what they do, and they don't either. I just know I can do it."

My Adam's apple bobs. "Can you change it back? Reverse it?"

He sighs, and his big breath causes me to hold my gag back. "I never tried before. Why you want it gone anyways? You the greatest weatherman ever."

I ruminate on this fact. I never wanted to be the greatest weatherman. Never wanted to receive awards. Never wanted to be hoisted above others. In second grade, a meteorologist visited the classroom. Dr. Mel was his name. He performed a wind simulation for the class, and I was fascinated. That night, I went on the internet and searched for how the weather does what it does. I carry that memory around with me each time I stand in front of a camera or my own phone.

I want people—no matter their age—to be as fascinated by the way the Earth works as I am. The planet is all we have, it's what keeps us moving. Being right about the weather is not what's important. It's giving the citizens a heads-up about an impending dangerous weather system. An F1 tornado is still a life-threatening storm, and the same safety precautions are in place if it were an F5.

"It's not about that," I say.

He speaks no words and walks behind me. He digs his fingers into my collarbones, and the trance returns. The man is dancing in front of me, with clothes this time. Then people of my past float by. My mother holding a mixing bowl and putting some elbow grease into the batter she always prepared. My father in the full suit he wore prior to heading to work. Mr. Terry sitting at his desk with his hands holding his head.

Then, the next morning comes. My teeth are chattering, and my body is convulsing. I leap from my bed and smile as I see the droves of people bundled in their winter gear. The plows are out frantically salting and sanding the ice-skating rinks that were the streams in the roads.

I shrug my winter coat on and before I know it, I am in the park. My plan is to speak with Mr. Terry and the rest of the Channel 8 news. I refuse to beg for my job back, but after a million sorrys, they must at least consider it.

As I cross the cement path, salt crunching under my boots, a woman is on the park bench. She has a cart filled with bottles and cans. Her life savings.

She is bundled in at least three blankets. She is in a deep sleep.

I reach into my pocket and remove a bundle of ten one-hundred-dollar bills and stuff them between her source of warmth, then I stand up and walk on.

That thousand dollars was the last of my savings. Even if it doesn't work out for me, I know I have a group of people on my side.

The clouds separate as I make my way up Whalley Avenue. The sun peeks through and shines down. A rainbow arcs through the sky, creating a perfect view.

That's something I could have never predicted.

Remembering Dr. Mel.

The Potato Peeler

Thanksgiving Day was always the biggest celebrated holiday in Sasha Greene's family history. A family member's death on Christmas Day twenty years ago essentially cancelled the holiday. December 25th caused a bulk of sadness for the family since that fateful day. New Years Eve was typically spent alone or only with their respective immediate household family members. But Thanksgiving was the one day a year when the entirety of the Greene family got together and had a feast. This year's was a bit different since the Harris family was joining the dinner.

Sasha and Michael met three years ago while Sasha was on a December girlfriends trip to New York City. On the Rockefeller ice skating rink, her best friend Monica was holding her hands since Sasha had never skated before and was absolutely terrified.

Monica guided her and set her free on her own for the first time. Sasha stayed upright, keeping her feet straight, and was enjoying the feeling of the cold wind in her face and the beautiful lights surrounding her. She was so mesmerized that she hadn't realized Monica was calling for her and giving instructions on how to turn. Sasha couldn't hear, and when the wall grew closer, turning and stopping would have come in handy.

All she could think to do was cover her eyes and brace for impact, so that was what she did. But there was no impact. She felt a pull on her puffy winter jacket and an arm around her waist. She looked up at this man—for some reason, her first thought was that he had a nice jawline. The beard scruff and mop of brown hair rounded out a good-looking man. He brought her to a stop and asked her if she wanted lessons.

Less than a year later, she could do a small jump, and they moved in together.

The Greene family thought it was a great idea to have Sasha and Michael host Thanksgiving dinner this year. Sasha was hesitant at first since this was always held at her parents' house, and her father's deep-fried turkey was the most succulent food she had ever eaten.

But before she could even get a word in, Michael said, "Oh, absolutely." She was a bit perturbed that he wouldn't talk to her first, but like through the extent of their relationship, when she was upset about something, she ignored it and filled Monica's phone with text bubbles while she cried quietly on the toilet. But she loved him for all the uplifting words he gave her every day. Especially the flowers and gifts she received for no special occasion, only because it was a Thursday.

Now she was in the kitchen where they ate so many meals together on the most important Thursday of the year. She sat at their small kitchen table with a potato peeler in hand, watching the brown skin slowly slide through the metal peeler and fall into the garbage pail beneath her. Homemade mashed potatoes were a Sasha Greene specialty, and her mother was counting on it.

Sweet childhood memories of waking up at 8 a.m. and peeling potatoes with her grandmother was how her dish came out perfect each and every time.

Michael was taking the turkey out of the oven and placing it on the stovetop. He needed to dress in a suit for his job every day, and he told her one time he felt uncomfortable in that type of attire. Sasha thought he looked sharp.

She was surprised to see he had a button down and a tie with slacks. It made her giddy that he was doing his best to impress her family.

Sasha enjoyed getting dressed up for any occasion she could. Even on a night out with friends, she would spend hours putting on makeup, curling her hair, and choosing the perfect outfit. For this Thanksgiving she chose a little black dress. It hugged her hips, and she liked the way it showed off her body. She had lost one hundred pounds since meeting Michael, and she was proud she could show off her toned physique. She thought the dress may have been too short for a family event, but she felt good about herself, and Michael agreed it was appropriate enough.

"The turkey is ready to serve," Michael said, turning to show the bird carved nicely into sections and placed neatly onto a large serving dish.

"That looks wonderful, dear. Mind if I—" She reached her hand out, and Michael slapped it away. It stung a bit, but his smile showed he was fooling around. She smiled back at him as he entered the dining room to place the turkey at the center of the long oval table Sasha had decorated with six individual name tags for their guests.

Sasha dumped the potatoes into the pot of boiling water. She never liked to cook, but Michael had a talent for the craft. She had told him many times that he should pursue that career, but he said he didn't like the restaurant business. Besides, he had a great paying job at the hedge fund.

While he readied the other foods, and her potatoes were ready to be mashed, he abandoned his chef duties to come up behind her and wrap his arms around her chest.

"You look so damn sexy in that dress," Michael said and gave a little bark in her ear. His hot breath on her neck and the kisses tenderly placed there were exciting her. If there was one thing he was better at than cooking, it was making love. And they did that often.

She enjoyed it and he most definitely enjoyed it. They had done it once this morning already, and their families were going to walk through the door any minute.

She shrugged him away and began using her elbow grease to pound the potatoes down into the pot after draining the water. But he wouldn't give up on his journey up her dress. In fact, he had invited himself in. His fingers were pulling her panties to the side and sliding a finger inside her. He could feel how wet she was, and that only made him more excited. He pulled the potato masher out of her hand and guided her to the round kitchen table. He bent her over the table, sliding her dress up, and her cheeks flopped out.

"Michael, my parents are going to be here any second." But he wasn't listening to anything she was saying. He was lost in his sexual world. It was always a look he had. The first time she saw it she thought he was having a seizure, but his movements were fluid, and what he was doing with his hands didn't indicate anything was wrong.

Her panties were at her knees now and she could hear the zipper to his pants going down. Then she felt what he had pulled out, probably just through the zipper hole. It slid easily inside of her, and it felt incredible. She had laid her head on the unsteady table and decided to bask in the pleasure. Until she heard the thunk of a car door slam. She tried to pull herself up, but Michael pushed her back down and kept driving inside of her.

"Michael, they're here. Stop it. My family is here." But he didn't stop. He didn't say a word. He only stared straight ahead in that trance. With his hand in the center of her back, it was impossible for her to move. Now the pleasure had gone away, not because her family—and his—were going to walk in on their porn scene, but because he had never been this aggressive before. She had never felt scared while making love to him before. But now she was scared, and she would think about this every time they made love. It was an important act to her, and now she wouldn't look at it the same.

Michael cried out a scattered pleasure moan, and she could feel a warm liquid flow inside her. He lifted her to a straight position, pulled her underwear back up, and pulled her dress back down over her ass just as there was a knock at the front door.

Michael opened the door and welcomed the guests inside with open arms. He had put the previous scene out of his head and was back to good ole kind, sweet Michael that the Greene family knew, and Sasha thought she knew, but now she was questioning the man she loved, and she didn't want to.

***

The gym was somewhere Sasha could escape her work, her family when they got out of hand, and just the world. Michael was with her at the 24/7 fitness center much of the time, but when he had a long day of work or was needed on a weekend or holiday, Sasha would go with Monica. Today was a Monica day since Michael's work claimed the day after Thanksgiving as a day of labor.

"How was your Thanksgiving?" Monica asked as they entered and scanned their keycards. Sasha loved hearing the clanking of the weights and the whoosh of the moving treadmills. Those were comfort sounds for her.

"It was—" She stopped, not sure how to describe the holiday. The time with her mother and father was magnificent. They talked about old memories and made new ones at that dinner table. Even hearing Michael's parents talk about him as a child and the mischievous things he would get into was a good, relaxing time. But she couldn't fully enjoy herself. All she was thinking about then and now was the event that preceded dinner. Even last night he wanted to go at it again, but she told him she had a headache, and he only shrugged and fell asleep. She saw that as a positive since he didn't force himself on her. "It was a good time."

"Really?"

"Really."

"Okay, but every year when I ask you about Thanksgiving, you go into a story of every word mentioned and how amazing it was. But all I get is 'a good time'?"

Monica was good at reading the emotions of not just Sasha but everyone they encountered. They used to play a game where Sasha would point at a person walking on the sidewalk, and Monica would have an entire life story and what they were going through just based on their gait and facial expressions. They never knew if it was true, but Sasha believed her every time.

They came ready to start their workout. They didn't carry a bag or anything other than car keys.

Their matching leggings and sports bra set were enough. As they were preparing to start, Sasha pulled Monica into the women's restroom. Half of the room was showers and lockers; the other half was toilet stalls.

Sasha pushed Monica into one of the showers and pulled the cellophane curtain closed.

"Uh, you know this looks really weird and it also may be illegal," Monica said.

"Shut up. And keep your voice down. I need to tell you something." Luckily, she only saw one woman by the sinks blow-drying her hair, so it was clear right now. "I—" She didn't know how to say this because she wasn't even sure what to call it. "Before my family came over, Michael had sex with me."

Monica's mouth was beginning to curl at the sides, and Sasha didn't blame her for smiling. A boyfriend and girlfriend making love was by society standards normal.

"I mean when I didn't want to."

"He raped you." Monica was always a loud one. Even her normal speaking voice was booming.

"Shut the fuck up," Sasha said through her teeth. But she saw Monica regretted her loudness when her hand cupped over her mouth. "I don't wanna call it that. I was enjoying it and fine with it, but my family was just outside, and they were going to walk in on us adding the wrong kind of juices to their mashed potatoes. I told him to stop because I was nervous, but he kept going. I—I don't know."

"Girl." Her voice was now at a safe indoor voice level. "You asked him to get up and he didn't, that's rape, honey."

"Yeah, but—"

Monica placed her index finger on her lip. "That is a sexual assault, and I am bringing you to the police station right now."

Before Sasha could make a sound, the shower curtain was ripped open, and they were heading for the exit.

The old woman standing in the locker area gave them a strange look, but there was no time for explanations.

***

"Stop it, Mon," Sasha said as she was guided to Monica's passenger seat. But the door was shut, and her friend started the car.

"No. He's going to prison. It's final," Monica said, pulling out of the fitness center parking lot.

"Wh—I don't want to press charges. What about that? I'm the one it happened to. And—besides, nothing even happened. We're overexaggerating."

"We?"

"Okay. I may have—be overblowing the whole thing."

Monica slammed the car's brakes when a yellow light switched to red. "So, you're saying he didn't rape you?"

Sasha exhaled a long breath she felt like she had been holding for a while. And even with the heat on full blast, she felt a chill rush up her back.

"I don't know. He's just always been so kind to me. I don't want to get him in trouble."

Sasha jumped when Monica slammed her hands on the steering wheel. She thought one of her acrylic nails would fly into the dashboard. "You're my best friend and I'm only doing this because I love you. My cousin was in the same situation with her boyfriend. He was tying her down and shit. It's personal for me."

Sasha ran her finger through her long blonde hair and dumped it over the headrest. "I'm sorry."

"You don't need to say you're sorry, you need to tell me we are reporting your boyfriend for rape."

Sasha's anxiety twisted her stomach into knots. She remembered reading so many articles about women who accused men of that act and were called a liar, a bitch, an attention-seeking whore. She didn't want to get pulled into that world.

"What if we just talk to him first? Like an intervention or something?"

Monica pulled the car to the side of the road and shoved the lever into park. "Really? An intervention? So, you want me and you to sit in a circle telling Mike what a dick he is?"

"No. I don't know. We're down the street. Just drop me off and I can pick up my car later. I'll talk with him when he gets home. Tell him how I feel."

Sasha's best friend shook her head in disgust but did as she said.

They sat in silence for the remainder of the ride.

It was uncomfortable to not hear Monica bitching about her family struggles and Sasha complaining about her work woes. Between the two of them, they constantly had something to say.

"What the fuck," Sasha said. A curse word so rare Monica gaped before her mouth fell farther open when she saw the provocation of the word.

As they ascended up the street, Michael was home and descending the steps, climbing into a white car Sasha didn't recognize.

They slumped in their seats as the car passed them by. Sasha caught a glimpse of the driver, a red-haired woman in a low-cut tank top with a chest the size of bowling balls.

"Maybe—" Sasha began.

"Maybe nothing. We're going to see for ourselves."

***

It was only a five-minute drive when the white Camry pulled into a driveway. It was a two-family home that was more tall than wide. They ran up the front steps side by side. Michael was swiveling his head as though the police were on his tail. If Sasha was the police, she would have tackled and cuffed him. Or just shot him dead. Sasha's heart jumped when the woman entered first and he guided her

125

inside by placing a hand inside the rear pocket of her blue jeggings.

"I know. I know," Monica said, comforting her crying friend.

"I don't understand. What did I do wrong?"

"Stop that shit right now. He's the one doing the wrong. The only fucking one. You hear me?"

Sasha nodded but still felt she must have said something or did something that chased him away from her.

"Just take me back to my car." Sasha's tone was full of grief. As though she had just lost a loved one. Which she had.

The ride back to the gym was more silent and awkward than the last one. She guessed it was different this time because Monica was at a loss of what to even say.

"Are you sure you don't want to stay with me? My little brothers are assholes, but my parents would welcome you with open arms."

Sasha feigned a smile and shook her head. "I gotta figure this one out on my own, thanks, though. Love you."

"Love you," Monica said.

When Sasha was back in her—their home, it felt gloomier and darker. All the lights in the place were glowing, but the light that burned bright from the love she felt was doused within seconds.

The living room where they shared laughs from the movie and TV show nights was now devoid of joy. The kitchen where they cooked many meals together was tainted by his act she was now convinced was rape. That memory played over and over like an old record.

Stop it.

She had said, *stop it.*

The bedroom. A place that once brought her great joy. The photo collage of her and Michael on an airplane before their Florida trip, Michael kissing her on the cheek. The photo of Michael holding her hands across the ice as though she were a small child. Three years of memories, three years of breaking, three years of mending. It all led to nothing.

And now she would lure him to that sacred place. Invite him into his own place. And have a little talk.

***

The leather nursing outfit was a getup that she had picked out to wear on his birthday a couple years ago. She thought she would feel powerful and sexy, but she just felt like a dope. It squeaked every time she moved an inch, which she was reminded of now as she crossed her bare legs.

The top was two openings designed for your breasts to hang out so your man could enjoy the view while you sat uncomfortably on top, or worse, underneath him.

She had enough time to curl her hair, put on a drag queen amount of makeup, and wander each room in her five-inch stiletto heels. That red-headed bitch was getting a longer session than she ever had in three years.

When he walked through the door, he looked haggard, and his skin was shimmering with sweat. He rounded the corner, looked up, and lost ten years within seconds. The way his grin grew to banana size and the way he threw his briefcase down, she knew she was in total control.

"What's the occasion?" he asked, moving closer.

"Just thought you deserved a nice relaxing time after your long night at work," she said as she rose. She stood a few inches taller than him in her shoes. It felt powerful.

She placed her arms around his shoulders and gave him a bit of a grind dance. He was enjoying himself. She could tell.

"Lie down," she said, inviting him to the bed.

He headed for the bed, but she put her arm out, blocking his way.

"What?" he said. A dopeish grin.

"You are forbidden to lie down while under the restrictions of clothing," she said, pecking him on the lips. A red stain remained, but he didn't notice, and his clothes were off in record time.

He lay down.

"Now spread out into an 'X' shape."

He did as he was told.

Sasha grabbed his right arm and restrained it inside a handcuff. She did the same to his left arm and both of his ankles, securing him to the bed frame.

"Now try to move."

He struggled and he was completely restricted. The metal restraint jangled against the metal frame.

"Now," she said, grabbing a cloth from the side table drawer. She placed it over his eyes. "Can you see?"

"No," he said with a dehydrated throat.

"Good." She grabbed the jelly from the drawer, though she needn't do any work. He was as strapped as a rocket ship ready for liftoff. Men were so easy to please. Like a puppy who spotted a chew toy from across the room. One boob and they were barking at your every whim.

She went to the end of the bed and knelt in front of the mushroom top. She guided her hand up and down, watching as he bucked and hollered at the immense pleasure he was feeling. She was feeling a type of pleasure too. Just not in the same way.

"You like that?" she asked, rolling her eyes.

"Oh my God, yes."

"Good, because here comes the best part."

She reached into the front pocket of the sexy nurse outfit and removed a potato peeler. The very same potato peeler she thought of each time the constant reminder of *stop it!* played through her head.

She gingerly stroked him with her left hand while her right hand controlled the slicer. She started just under the tip, positioning the blade so the full shaft got a dose of the action.

As she led the peeler down, his shouts of joy turned into shouts of pain. The skin ripped off just as the skin of the potato had. Her joy grew watching the blood dribble and paint a pretty picture across his hairy testicles. His bucking and hawing body in the restraints was a sight to witness. If they had downstairs neighbors, they may have thought they were getting a good fuck. But tonight was for Sasha. A night made for her.

"What the fuck are you doing?" Michael's whiny, pathetic voice called out. His tears were as real as the ones she spread, not just Thanksgiving night or earlier today, but the buildup of little disagreements throughout the relationship that were put into perspective by one action from the man tied to the bed. "Ah, stop it. Stop it, please."

She peeled the opposite side down to the balls, until the blood made it impossible to make out a base from a shaft from a tip.

She stood and dropped the peeler back into the front pocket.

"Sorry, hon. This nurse is off duty. Maybe the woman whose house you just left can help you out."

His eyes were still covered, but his body had stopped moving.

She wasn't sure if he was dead, and she didn't much care to know.

She unclasped her heels, threw them back into the closet. Unzipped her uniform, hung it on the hanger it started on. She took a shower, threw on a tank top, leggings, and sneakers. She took one last look at the pathetic hunk of flesh that had caused so much anguish for her. Limp, bloodied, and a useless item that continued to pump red instead of white.

She didn't need much else.

She walked until she reached the bus station, and she would travel to a place she hadn't decided on yet.

Start somewhere new with somebody new.

Somebody who would love her and treat her with respect. Not a difficult concept some just couldn't grasp.

As she walked, she wondered what Monica would think of her best friend. Though, Sasha imagined, she would soon find out.

As the fluorescent lights grew closer in the early hours of the morning, she chose a destination, paid with the money she took from Michael's wallet, and found an empty seat on the nearly deserted bus. All she had was her purse, the clothes on her back, and her trusty potato peeler.

For the women who have never been shown respect. You deserve love.

Our Flesh is the Same

The cage grew smaller with each second that passed. It began as a box wide enough to fit my naked body and the space forced me to my knees and elbows, but now my forearms and shins were aching more with each passing second. I stared through the bars at the sickeningly white exterior space, my clean-shaven flesh cold against the metal bottom.

Blue plastic chairs on top of four metal legs neatly lined in three rows, facing away from me and at a television perched in the top left corner. I had seen them come in, waiting in those chairs with one of us either already dead or being handed off for decimation.

The constant retching, the constant weak whimpers, soft so the boss didn't come with the prongs to quiet us, the constant sniffles reminding me of the brains we held true inside us all. Being trapped was not what defined us, but what we once were on the outside.

My cage neighbor was quite talkative when the lights went out. Darkness meant the noise levels could rise and unfortunately when the bottled-up feelings could be let out. Any release from what we kept internally was good for the body, mind, and soul. As we all awaited the terrors we witnessed many times throughout the day, the more we agreed we looked forward to our turn in the slaughterhouse.

"A special report from the president will begin momentarily," the news reporter on the television stated at top volume.

The boss and the crew were out on a run, which meant the sounds we made from our cages were minute compared to the wails and cries of what was found.

"It is not clear what the president will state in the address, but what we do know is there appears to be a major break in the bill that has been sitting on the president's desk for a month. A bill that if signed will affect slughterh—" The reporter paused and held a hoof to its ear. "Here is the president now."

The chambers were filled with members of congress and the house. Long noses, twitching ears, loud huffs, and trills from the mixed batch. A separation of two sides with our lives in the hands of those who would work together based on their feelings that would benefit themselves.

A click of footsteps panned the president across the stage and to the podium. The beady eyes took a second to scan the chambers, to take it all in and wait for the half applause to simmer down before beginning.

Flittering triangle folded ears, a snout ending with two breathing holes wiggled, and the president said, "Vice president, speaker, constituents, and citizens across this great country, I'm sure you are all wondering why I have called this conference here today." Vice President released a whinny and sent the mane flying with a shake of excitement. Speaker's fur shimmered with pride in the well-lit chambers.

Shrieks sent me back to the white room and the unpleasantness on the outside. The front metal door burst open, and the pain of the woman could be felt in my bones. "Stop. Please. I didn't do anything wrong. Why are you doing this?"

Sharpened claws of the boss's crew dug into the women's arms, blood streaked and dripped from her fingertips, giving the negative space some color. A familiar color—we in our cages were far too familiar with what came next.

"A bill was passed by the house and congress and landed on my desk some time ago. I am sure the citizens are curious about my decision." The president's calm demeanor competed with the women's screams of terror in the slaughter room.

Her nude body was tossed on the table by the boss's do-gooders. The boss clomped through the door and pointed, giving direction of what to do next without uttering a word.

"Please don't hurt me or my baby. Don't fucking touch my fucking baby, you disgusting pigs. This is my body, and you don't get to—"

Her words were cut short by a muzzle strapped to the back of her skull. She still spoke, but a quiet, muffled grunt was all that came through.

"I can't stand the noises they make. It's unbearable," one of the crew said, grabbing a belt embedded in the metal table. Droplets of red filled the table from the claw marks, a small dose of what was to come.

"My decision did not come lightly," the president continued. "These are creatures with brains, blood, and a heart. A heart that lives within each and every citizen in this country. And I know some of you will disagree. This has been a hot button issue for years. Citizens showing their passion with picket signs outside of the slaughterhouses."

"Damn fucking right," the boss said. "Trying to take our jobs away and shut us down."

I had to get out of this cage. It was a thought I had that never left my consciousness. I had a family on the outside. Children who were growing and excited for their futures. When the boss picked me up, I was by myself, and I wondered where they were now. And if they still were.

The body of the woman listed and bucked as she was fully strapped to the table. Whimpers in solidarity from my neighbor and from the five others in their embedded cages in the wall could be heard and wouldn't be silenced when a slaughter was in progress.

"Think about what you're doing," a voice from the cage a few down said.

"She probably has a family," my neighbor added.

"This is murder," I chimed in.

"Shit. I wish we could muzzle all these stupid fucking animals," one of the crew said as he removed a machete from a drawer.

This was the final straw. I had witnessed too many massacres. I couldn't handle watching person after person slaughtered before my very eyes. My shoulder was shot with pain when I rammed it against the cage. The yells of the woman on the table masked my attempt to break free.

"And I hear all the cries, and I read all the letters I receive," the president said. "However, this meat is our survival. We are carnivores and cannot survive without this source of vitamins and minerals. In addition, these slaughterhouses are creating jobs, and what a loss in the economy it would be if it all were shut down."

On the third shoulder shove, I was beginning to think there was no escaping.

"Ready the slide," a crew said, and the other pulled a metal slide, positioning it at the end of the table where the woman's legs were forcibly spread, her vagina full of dark hairs and the crown of a head splitting the walls. However, the way the child exited was not up to the mother.

This method was repeated many times every day. Whether it was somebody the crew found on their own or dropped off by one of them, the process was the same. Children were at the top of their priority list. Fresh meat tasted the best according to them. When released, the child would be killed and placed in the cold storage locked in the rear of the slaughterhouse.

"Ready to go," the crew said, and the boss watched on, paws crossed on a barrel chest, ready for the slaughter.

Hoarseness took over the woman's sounds. She was tired of trying and made it easy for the crew to position the blade in the center of her bulging stomach.

Another shove on the cage and progress this time. One of the bolts holding the hinge dropped inside with me, and I was sure one more shoulder into the cage would send it to the floor.

"I am signing this bill into law," the president said. "Slaughterhouses will continue to operate, and the production of meat will remain domestic and fresh. And with this law comes the legality of hunting your own meat. Using approved hunting rifles, every citizen will have the right to execute these creatures and use them for consumption. Trophy kills remain prohibited."

The blade slid through the distended stomach starting at the breastbone and slicing down to the clitoris. The stomach was pulled open by the claws of justice, and the fresh meat slid out. The umbilical cord attached to the baby's navel was disconnected by bared teeth. The slide sent the child into the paws of the boss. Cries from the baby made my decision final.

The cage door flew halfway across the room, and I followed out of my prison cell without immediately wondering what the reactions of the two crew and the boss were. Without thought, the crew were after me.

My back took some time to straighten out and my legs tingled, shooting up and down my nerves. Running out the door was my only shot at freedom. A freedom I had once before, and seeing the reddened baby, hearing its scared cries, I'm reminded of my own family and a reunion that was not expected but the newborn child a human savior to begin anew.

"I hope for the citizens of this country to be civil in my decision and respect one another's opinions on the matter," the president said. "I will leave you with this. Survival is all we have in this short life; why not make it as simple as possible for all?"

I made a dash at the child, which confused both of the crew. The boss stood guard of the child and showed off the bloodied teeth that separated the child from their mother. Their mother who lay motionless on her final resting place, split open, breasts exposed, and the final image of what we were to all of them. A piece of flesh not required for their survival and not giving us the option of our survival.

One of the crew went to the floor fast when I kicked the knee, slipping trying to regain balance as the other crew ran. Using the slick floor of blood to my advantage, I stepped to the side. The other crew went into the wall, and as I approached the boss, I snagged the machete off the table.

"You don't understand a word I'm saying," I said. "But just know that we are living, breathing beings that are not for your sole consumption. Legal or not. Now if you take one step toward me, I will cut your fucking head off."

"God bless everybody," the president said.

One swing was all it took for the machete to enter halfway into the boss's neck. Those huge pupils couldn't decide whether they would stay large or shrink to nothing. Death made its rounds in the boss's head. The boss was on the floor, machete still in the meaty neck that looked good enough to eat.

"And God bless these United States of America."

I hugged the child close; its cries seemed to simmer when held to my skin. The machete was easy to remove from the now dead body, and the blade waved the two crew back on their paws, enough to subdue them and escape.

Trees huddled in the distance beyond the diamond chain-link fence surrounding the outside of my prison.

"Get the fuck back here." One of the crew found the bravery to come after me, but I wouldn't let the paws get close.

I ran to the fence with the machete swinging in my right hand and protecting the child with all my heart. Running along the interior, I discovered a cut-out for entering and exiting. I used my shoulder once more to break through and into the safety of the woods. The crew wouldn't chase after. This was where we ruled over them and they were scared. The blood I was covered in was one of theirs. This would be in their head forever, knowing that we fight back, and we would win every single time.

For those who are being thrown around by the powers that be.

The Pizza Cult

The reverberation of the metal door worried me that any persons on Wooster Street could hear my knuckle raps. A quick scan proved that nobody was in sight. Businesses lined this narrow road including a laundromat, a convenience store—not 24 hours— and an independent bookstore. If this were the morning on a weekend, the street would be filled with eager shoppers picking up their needs and wants for the upcoming week, but this was three in the morning. The silence was equal parts an eerie and calming feeling.

An autumn wind was strong between the buildings on both sides, creating a wind tunnel and blowing my shoulder-length hair into a tizzy. The hand holding the manilla envelope was growing colder with each gust, my other hand keeping warm in my hoodie front pocket.

I was familiar with this part of the city: directly across from the meeting point was O'Malley's pub where I had frequented for three years, becoming a regular with my order sitting on the bar top before I reached my seat. But an incident with an ex-girlfriend involved me swinging my fist, inadvertently striking the owner trying to break up the fight, which had earned me a permanent ban from the establishment. An arrest from the incident began a domino effect for me. Lost my job, lost my home, lost my love for everything. And now standing outside this door was the opening I needed to turn my life around.

My ears hurt from the screech of a sliding peephole opening in the middle of the door. Green eyes showed through, and a voice said, "Password?"

"Uh, no char, keep it thin," I said.

The eyes disappeared and were replaced with the thunk of a lock disengaging and an ajar door. This seemed like my invitation to enter, but before I did, I checked my surroundings, happy I wasn't spotted as I stepped inside.

"Close the door and lock it," a voice from the dark called. It was a more aggressive welcoming than I was expecting.

After doing what I was told, I worked my way slowly into the small space. Cigarette stench permeated the air, mixed with beer that had spilled years ago and was never cleaned.

"Is it possible to turn a—"

Before I could ask, a light clicked on and there were more bodies than I expected. Two men sat at a poker table, and I say poker because the river was about to be dealt, and each guy had two cards face down. One stood feet away from me as though he were ready to show an open house on the 10x10 basement space.

"I would invite you to join, but we're already too deep into this game. Name's Rob," the man who opened the door said and stuck a hand to shake in my direction. I took it, and he held on while introducing the other two. "The one with the porn stache is Gary, and the one with the lazy eye is Mark. Sorry for the normie names. Our mothers were all different and clearly unoriginal."

"Hey," Mark said. "My momma named me after Marky Mark. She saw that underwear ad after my pops left her with me growing inside, and she fell in love."

Rob grabbed a steel folding chair and placed it out, motioning for me to join the group.

"My dad named me Gary because I'm number five in a long line of Gary's. I went to the state to change it, and my dad followed me there and had to physically remove me from the probate court building. I hate traditions and my name. Anyway, that was last week and here we are."

All three of them looked to be in their twenties, maybe early thirties, so me approaching thirty myself settled my uneasy feeling a bit.

"So, you got the goods?" Rob asked, taking a seat. The three men picked up their cards, and Rob laid out the river card.

"Ah, you fucking bastard," Gary yelled, smacking the table. "I needed a three of clubs and you throw down a diamond, you fucking bastard."

"You know you're supposed to have a poker face playing poker, right?" Mark said.

"Ah, whatever. I fold and I'm grabbing another beer. Hey, new kid, you want one?"

I zoned out for a minute after placing the manilla envelope on the table, as though it was ready to be gambled away with the mountain of multi-colored chips in the center of the table. "Ah, no, thanks," I said.

"What are you, one of those dry fellas?" Gary asked.

"No," I said, without any harshness. "The drink was just the start of the downhill of my life."

"Yeah, my uncle was hooked on whiskey, and one night we found him in a bush trying to make it grow with his piss," Mark said.

"Hey, that's fair. I don't judge nobody."

"Anyway, sorry about Gary," Rob said, staring at me. "Place your cards down, Mark."

The two remaining guys placed the cards face up.

"A flush beats…uh, nothing," Mark said.

"I was trying to bluff, but old Gary made a big show out of the cards."

"Ah, fuck you, Robby. You were gonna lose either way."

"I'll get you in the next round, Mark."

As Mark collected his winnings, Rob took the envelope and unwound the red string to open the top flap. He pulled out the three papers and spread them evenly where the winning chips were laid.

"Oh, this is good. Good shit," Rob said.

Gary reached across after slinging down half his beer and snatched the papers to read. "How did you get this if you don't mind me askin'?"

"Uh, well—"

"You don't need to reveal that information," Rob said.

"Yeah, as we should have pointed out from the start," Mark said. "Don't mind Gary. He's a little..." Mark put a thumb to his mouth and pinky in the air, tilting his finger bottle back.

"Fuck you, Marky. You drink more than me."

The comment was met with a double eyeroll from both Mark and Rob.

"The bottom line is," Rob began, "this will be what we need to put old Franky out of business."

"We are not putting him out of business, but we certainly are going to steal most of his customers," Mark said.

Franky's place had been a staple in this city for going on forty years, and I worked for him for three of those years. It was the best job I ever had. I would get there at 5:43 a.m. each morning and start the dough. As the dough was in the rising stage, I would make the sauce. When the sauce was finished, I would prep toppings and salads for the day. I was doing more work than any server, cook, or even Franky himself.

Then the arrest came, and he couldn't handle the bad press for his place of business. When I was released from jail a day later and forced one year probation, I was no longer on the payroll and was replaced that same day. No phone calls, no text message, no house visit. I showed up for my shift and my key didn't work in the back door. Then fifteen minutes later, a teenage boy wandered past me, and his key fit was flawless. Franky called a week later and apologized for the way the firing was handled. I told him to "fuck right on off. You and your mother." The mother part was harsh, but it was the worst time of my life, and I was fed up with existence.

The following weeks were hell. I applied to every pizza place in the city and never heard back from one. The thing about Franky was that he had major pull in the city. Speculation told me he contacted every other pizza joint and gave them the rundown of what he thought of me. It had to be the mother comment that made him upset. His mom had been dead twenty years at that point.

Following getting booted from my apartment because the fast-food job wasn't bringing in the money I needed to pay rent, I crashed at my ex-girlfriend's apartment—yes, the one I swung at—but when she got a new boyfriend, it became an even more awkward situation. I stayed at homeless shelters until one guy very proudly shouted that he had the urge to choke me to death in my sleep. One night I even stayed at a motel, but one bedbug scurrying across my thigh was enough for me to leave an hour after check-in.

At a loss, I tried the internet to see if there was anybody in a similar situation, and maybe if they came out clean on the other side, I could too. One hour access to the library computer was ten dollars and the last ten dollars I had until the next pay period. I read through articles giving advice on how to make money fast. I was smart enough to not fall for a get-rich-quick scam, but when a Reddit link showed up on my Google search, it felt like a jackpot moment. The heading read: *Looking for information on big pizza joint.*

My body went stiff and I couldn't click on the page fast enough. My hour had been up for five minutes. I could feel the librarian's stare burning the back of my head. But I had to know. It explained that this guy was starting up a new pizza joint and wanted to be the best. And it read, "*to beat the best, you have to be the best. So, if you know info on the best, reach out to me.*" I knew what this redditor wanted and sent them a personal message with the phone number to my shitty flip phone and to call at any time. Before I could take one step outside the library, Rob called. He wanted the Franky's dough recipe, the sauce recipe, even where they got the toppings. When payday came around, I returned to the library and wrote out the recipe I knew by heart and photocopied the pages at ten cents a page. I showed up at their door at the agreed upon time of three in the morning in the basement of the in-progress pizza joint.

"You doin' okay, kid?" Gary asked, concern heard for the first time.

"Oh, yeah. I'm good. I just hope this works out," I said.

Then there was quiet. Exhaustion was creeping up when, before arriving here, I lay in a different shelter and unable to sleep, but now it was taking charge and pressing weight on my eyelids. Mark's lazy eye was drifting left, and I wondered if that was what happened when he was tired. Gary leaned back in his wood chair, and the squeaks sounded like cries before the legs would snap from beneath his beer belly body. Rob had hair, and it looked nice sitting atop his oval head; he adjusted the top piece to swoop to the side. All three sets of eyes were on me, maybe minus one of Mark's.

"So, now that you have that, I can take my money and go," I said. My heart was racing at the prospect of money in my bank account, at asking for the money in this basement at three thirty in the morning.

"Hm, well, that will take some time," Rob said, standing and stretching.

My racing heart skipped a few beats and my stomach flopped. I quit my fast-food job and promised a first month's rent of a new apartment downtown to a relator.

"You told me over the phone that I would be paid handsomely. Those are your exact words, Rob."

Mark and Gary rose and stood behind Rob, who paused them with a wave of his hand. As if to say he could handle me just fine. "You are correct. Those were my exact words, but I did not say when. When we open upstairs and are sitting comfortably in our business, then sure, you will be paid a large amount, as this is your recipe. Well…not yours, but regardless. Be patient. Maybe a year from now, you will be swimming in hundred-dollar bills."

I stepped forward and reached for the papers: the only thing giving this place a chance to survive in the clustered pizza city of the world. Gary slid the papers off the table, and they floated to the floor. The words on the paper didn't matter so much to me. I could write the same words a million times. But they didn't deserve my work if I wasn't paid upfront.

"This is bullshit. Give it to me or pay me. Those are your two options," I said.

Rob's hands were pressing down on my shoulders, and then he shoved me. It was so unexpected I had no time for balance, and I was on my ass before Gary collected the papers. Joined by Mark and Rob, they were up the front stairs and gone.

I chased but when I reached the top, the door was locked. I pounded on the door, most likely leading into the unready restaurant. "Give me my shit back," I demanded, followed by many more knocks. It was no use. They were already, if they were smart, entering the information onto a computer and saving it to a hard drive or thumb drive.

There was a time in the midst of the job loss, apartment loss, and girlfriend loss that I considered opening my own place with Franky's recipe. But I quickly learned that a lot of money was required to open a business. And I had none. Now I had less.

And those three fuckers stole it from me. They took a shot in the dark on the internet and hoped they would cash in on some dumbass who would bring them the recipe for the largest pizza joint in the city. And they found their dumbass. Me.

Instead of wallowing in my emptiness, I exited the way I came. The scream of the door hinges would have given me away, but I peered left and right in case the three doofuses were waiting for me.

The street was clear, and I shut the door with the quietest ease. Not possible with the hunk of metal. With a sense of curiosity and rage, I stepped to the right and pressed my palms to the window of the storefront that was meant to be the next Franky's. Through the shadows and with nature's lighting, it was clear there was no restaurant going there. Inside was a dining hall. Nothing but round wood tables with folding chairs leaned against each set up. A stage was at the far end of the room, and two speakers bookended the space intended for a band or a guest of honor.

"What the fuck is going on?" I muttered to myself.

Headlights swept around the corner and down the one-way street. It was early, but it wasn't unusual for a car to pass by. Or in this case a minivan. The door slid open, and soccer mom jokes ran through my mind as a hood was placed over my head and I became the next contestant on "kidnapped in the big city."

***

The hood was snatched off, and familiarity flooded my senses before my brain could catch up with the actual danger I may have been in. The table with playing cards, the stench of dried-up barley and cigs, men's eyes staring at me as though I was the star of the stage play I was forced into.

I was in that van for fifteen minutes; did they just circle downtown until they felt I was disoriented enough to be released of my blindness and misremember spending the last hour in this very basement? There was no rope binding me to the same steel chair that hurt my bum after a while, and the door to Wooster Street was clear and open. If I wasn't a prisoner or being kidnapped, then what the fuck was happening?

"Hello, Danny boy," the mustached man in front of me said. It wasn't the porn stache guy named Gary who stood in the background with lazy eyed Mark and Rob, who I thought was running the operation, but there was a new character in this story, and I knew exactly who the man was.

"Franky, long time no see. You went through the trouble of kidnapping me but couldn't dial a measly phone number to fire me all those months ago?"

"Hey, nobody is kidnapped. You can walk right out that door and I or any of my friends won't stop you."

"Then why was a spit guard thrown over my face, and why was I shoved into a van?"

"For some pizazz."

If pizazz was what old Franky wanted, I would happily pizazz him right in the fucking face. "What is all this? And give me a real answer."

"We just want to open a pizza place and—"

Rob was cut short by Franky. "Shut up, Robby." Franky would always end everyone's name with a "Y" no matter what the name was. Danny, Marky, Christina-y. "This was a test."

A minute of silence felt like an hour, waiting for more explanation, but of course I had to be the one to talk. "Fucking continue. What test? You're talking to me like I'm in on the joke, but the punchline is not tickling me."

"You answered the internet thing my boys put up to see if any of my former employees would spill the beans of my recipe I entrusted them with."

The burst of laughter that came from my chest surprised even myself. "Are you fucking serious?"

"I'm afraid so, Danny boy. And it looks like you failed."

"Failed big time," Gary yelled from the back, still holding a stack of playing cards in his hand like he was ready to perform a magic trick. His bald head, most likely shaved off to prevent premature balding, looked like a magic 8 ball I would like to shake and predict my future. Was I going to get out of here alive? *Don't count on it.*

"Then get to the good part already. What happens next? You gonna take out a gun and end my life for revealing the most basic pizza recipe on this earth? Be real right now, Franky."

"That's not what this is about. I want to make you money since I know you're struggling."

"Fuck you, Franky. Fuck you right up the ass," I said proudly.

"So, you don't need money then?"

Speaking of ass, I stood up because mine was about to shatter into a million pieces. "You fire me and months later show up telling me I need money. Great detective skills, Sherlock Holmes. Why don't you get one of your Watson's in the back to take you back to elementary school with your keen eye for the details."

"You always were a wise ass. I liked that about you, but your wisecracks were what got you into trouble. But to bring us to the here and now, I want you to have money. And lots of it."

Struggling to find a place to rest my head each night, looking in recycling bins for cans and bottles at ten cents apiece, and scrouging food wherever I could get it even on a fast-food worker's hourly rate was getting old fast. I was desperate, which was why I was in front of these four fools.

"Do you do this to all your former employees or—"

Uncomfortable shuffling of Gary's feet, Mark scanning the entire room all at once, and Rob picking the skin of his cuticles answered the question for me.

"What do I need to do?" I said.

The full, bushy, black—with a ton of help from hair dye—mustache bristled, and that was the scariest thing I had experienced up to that point.

"We got a call from a former employee," Franky continued. "You might know him, Justin, who is happily willing to give over my recipe. All you need to do is pick him up from his house because he's too young to drive and bring him here."

The kid who had the new keys the day I found out I no longer held a job. The teenager who took my spot as dough maker. "And let me guess, you fired him, and he's upset about it, so to get you back, he's giving away the recipe."

"Sound familiar?"

"And if I do this, then what? I'm part of your crew here?"

"You do this, I will hand you a grand stack."

A thousand wasn't a ton of money, but it was what I needed to get a nice place to stay for a bit, and if he was offering more for other jobs, I would be back in an apartment in no time.

"As you may know," I said, "I don't have a car, so—"

Car keys were flying at me before I could finish my thought.

"Do not put a scratch anywhere on my baby. And for the love of all things holy, do not get pulled over."

With a salute to Franky and the three stooges, I was off into the early morning light. Would I return? Wouldn't they like to know.

***

The teen lived in a nice neighborhood. It must've been a thirty-minute commute for his mom to drop him off early each morning. And didn't the kid go to school? Maybe he was one of those homeschooled kids. Either way, I just wanted to take this kid back to the city to collect my thousand dollars.

No contact information was handed off to me. Just an address that I sat outside of with no lights on inside and no movement. It was something to look at, though. The lawn was immaculate. It was cut like the outfield of Yankee stadium. The house was a two-story brick monstrosity. If his parents were rich out the wazoo, then why the fuck was his mom driving him to one of the most dangerous cities in the United States to work at a pizza joint for just above minimum wage? At least I had the excuse that I was poorer than an Italian not part of the mob.

If I carried a weapon, I would have shot through the passenger side window at the sound of pulling at my door handle. It wasn't mine; it was Franky's minivan he was so protective over.

"Give me a fucking minute," I said. The last car I owned had crank handles to roll the windows down and up, and the locks had to be manually pulled up to open. So, all the electronic buttons were no clearer than when my Italian grandmother would speak in our native language with me having no interest in learning. A disgrace to our heritage is what I was.

After moving the side mirrors and rolling down a couple windows, I found the unlock button so the kid could climb in. His military cut and cleanly pressed clothes made him more intimidating than before.

"You scared the shit out of me, kid," I said.

"I had to sneak out the back so my mom wouldn't see me leaving. Sorry."

I held hatred for this kid for taking my job, but hearing him speak in the closeness of the car opened my eyes to how young he truly was.

"Your family rich or something?" I asked.

The kid turned away as though he was seeing his house for the first time and said, "Something."

We didn't speak almost the entire way back to the city until my curiosity kicked in. "If you got a big house like that, then why were you working a job so far from home?"

He narrowed his eyes, and his bushy eyebrows inverted at me. "We're not a normal family." And he coldly turned away.

Any interaction I had with teens in the homeless shelters were similar answers to this one. I was interested in their life, and they wouldn't talk about it. But this teen seemed different, like he wanted to escape to another world. But didn't we all want to do that?

Two full minutes passed from pulling up to the outside of the door behind which Franky, Rob, Gary, and Mark were most likely waiting for the arrival of their new candidate. But he wasn't moving or talking. "You ready to—"

"No."

Fear shot through my body when he reached into his waistband and removed a revolver. "What the fuck are you doing with that, dude?" I reached for the door handle, but the barrel was on me.

"Don't leave this car. If you do, I don't mind putting one right between your eyes." The coldness coming from a kid was more menacing than any other human holding a firearm. The scariest part of the interaction was that I believed him.

"Hey, nobody's leaving anywhere," I said, raising my arms like a criminal. "Maybe if you told me what was on your mind, I could possibly hel—"

"You talk too fucking much," the kid said. "The truth of the matter is you don't wanna know. The truth is I was given instruction to kill you right here in this van."

I felt a but coming; was there a but coming?

"But," he said, "I'm not going to do that. Do you know why?"

"Because you are a good kid."

"Fuck no. I've been in juvie five times for so many things you only dream you could do."

There was no doubt I dreamed of robbing a bank or breaking into a home like the one the kid exited, but I viewed myself as a stand-up citizen, always doing things the correct way. The legal way. Being a foster kid shot through the system, never being a correct fit for any family, did two things: built thick skin and made me watch other struggling kids make bad decisions. I never judged them because if I didn't have the job at Franky's at the right time, I would be in prison instead of the driver's seat of a minivan with a gun pointed at me.

"I stopped listening to my dad a while ago," the kid said and, being swept up in my own memories, I half heard what he said.

"Your dad?"

"Yeah. You work for him," the kid said in this condescending tone that would have pissed me off in any other case, but this news was groundbreaking.

"So, this was a trap from the beginning," I said more to myself than the kid.

"He's super obsessed and paranoid about his precious pizza place and being the best in the world and nobody stealing his precious recipe. He started this obsession with three of his friends that he would take out anybody who knew the recipe."

So, after the firing was the beginning of the end for me. If I never answered the online forum, he would have eventually found me and brought me to his lair on Wooster Street. But me coming by myself under my own power was an easy way to make me disappear. Especially somebody like me who had lost everything in their life.

"He was a horrible father. Never there to teach me right from wrong or play catch with me, even though I hate sports," the kid continued. "It was always the restaurant. And when he fires somebody, he puts me, the teenager, in their place to really get under their skin, so they would be angry enough to openly give away the recipe to losers online."

"How many people has he done this to?" I asked.

"Really? That's your question? You're the second one. The first guy made me not want to kill another person ever again, but I did it because he's my dad. But matching blood doesn't mean anything when he was never a father. And now his blood is gonna drain out."

He reached for the door handle, and I opened my mouth to stop him but snapped it shut. What words would I use to stop an angry kid from destroying a figure that had stood in his way from the conception of his life? Never knowing my parents left me with a sour taste, and never having parents through the foster system made that taste unbearable. I never had help from anyone, which made me rely on others for things I never knew. Which made me trust others less and less to the point of living in my own existence and only helping myself.

And as the kid opened the door and the first shot rang out, I shifted the van into drive and planned on pressing the gas pedal until the wheels went bald.

For Tom & Lia.

The Evil Car

CHAPTER 1

The evil car wasn't ruining the life of Brian Collins yet. The evil car was in the hands of an old man in Jackson, Mississippi. That old man was going to pass it off to his friend in Atlanta, Georgia. She was going to hand it off to a family member in Scranton, Pennsylvania. That family member would then pass it along to his old football coach, Kevin Collins.

The reasons each previous owner had for wanting to be rid of the hunk of metal were unknown to those to whom it was passed on. But they would soon find out. Brian Collins would soon find out.

***

"Throw it back," Brian said.

The spiraling football hit his hands with a *thwack*. Oliver Jones had the best arm in the state, and all his friends knew because he never stopped talking about it.

"I'm telling you, Brian. I'm going to play professionally," Oliver said now, receiving the ball from Brian.

"And I'm telling you to stop talking about it. Has your mom never told you that if you say a wish out loud it won't come true?" Brian said.

"My mom is dead. And you know that."

Brian had to stop from cracking a smile. Brian's mother had died also, three years ago. It was a never-ending cycle of blabber between the two boys. It was something they could bond over, despite the sadness of the subject.

"At least you have me," Brian said, sailing the ball over Oliver's head and into the Jeffersons' yard.

"Yeah, but I'm glad you're not quarterbacking on Friday nights," Oliver said.

Mr. Jefferson stepped out the front door immediately. "What did I tell you boys. Play in the street; it's a cul de sac for cripes' sake." He slammed the door as Oliver jogged back over into the safety of the Collins's yellowed grass caused by the previous winter's destruction.

"What is wrong with that guy?" Oliver asked.

"I don't know. Ever since he moved in two months ago, he has been so angry. He never even came over to say hello."

"He must have a stick up his ass," Oliver said.

The boys shared a laugh until the Jeffersons' front door opened again. But it wasn't Mr. Jefferson. It was Alaina. His daughter.

Brian followed her from her red Converse low-tops to her maroon plaid skirt to her white crop top to her straight black hair resting at her shoulders.

When her brown eyes glanced at the two glaring teenage boys, Brian shoved the football into Oliver's stomach. Oliver let out an *umph* and then did the same back to Brian. Brian chased Oliver through the yard until Alaina was around the corner and out of view.

"You idiot," Brian said.

"Me? You were the one drooling all over yourself."

"I was not drooling."

"Yes, you were. Look." Brian held his pointer finger to Oliver's chest.

Oliver looked down and Brian flicked him in his big nose, nearly entering nostril territory.

Brian took off into his house and shut the door before Oliver could enter.

"Off limits," Brian said.

"So, we're done hanging?"

"I've got homework to finish."

"It's Friday."

"And I want to get it done now so I can actually enjoy my weekend."

Oliver huffed. "Fine. Still on for tomorrow?"

"Can't until the afternoon. Got my driver's test in the morning."

"Oh, so you can take Alaina on a hot date," Oliver said mockingly.

Oliver was close enough to the screen door to where Brian bopped him on the nose again.

"If you break my nose, you can explain to my dad how you were 'just clowning around.'"

"I'm not even close to breaking it. But if you want me to—"

"Go do your homework, nerd," Oliver said, stepping off Brian's stoop.

When Oliver was far enough away for his ears to hear, Brian said, "Yeah, sure, my homework.

CHAPTER 2

"So, let's see here. You backed into a curb, ran a stop sign, nearly hit an elderly lady crossing the street in a crosswalk where you failed to yield, and turned right on red when you weren't supposed to."

The driving instructor ticked off the violations on his clipboard that Brian committed during the test for his license. Brian was sure he was going to receive a failure and would need to try again. He passed the written test, getting only one question wrong, but he was a great test taker. He had a specialty of passing a test, be it science, math, or history even if he failed to study the days prior. Oliver called him the "testing wizard." But getting into the car and driving didn't use the type of brain power Brian had.

"Luckily for you, I've seen worse. Much, much worse. Congratulations, you pass," the plain-looking man said, handing Brian a plastic, rectangular card ensuring he could climb behind the wheel of a car and go. He held freedom and wonder in the palm of his hands.

"You will go between home and school. And that's it," his father scolded when they arrived back home.

"What about to Oliver's house?" Oliver lived directly next door, but he wanted to roll up in his hot rod that didn't exist as of yet.

His dad snickered. "Oliver's is fine, but don't push it further."

"Oh, I also don't even have a car to drive anywhere," Brian said.

"I—you leave that up to me."

"Wait, does that mean you're getting me a car?" His excitement was growing.

"It means you will need to wait and see."

Brian jumped, raising his fist into the air. "Yes." And he ran up to his room.

Brian lay on his bed and daydreamed about cruising around town, pulling into the shake shop and seeing Alaina at the counter.

"Can I buy you a Grande Vanilla Shake?"

"Oh, yes, please. My hero."

A tap at his window snapped him from his fantasy. Another tap right after. Oliver was in his back yard, throwing pebbles at his window.

Brian flung the window open and said, "What?"

He could see something different in Oliver's face. His usual flawless hair that hung perfectly over his eyebrows was disheveled and pointing in all haphazard directions. His hands were on his knees, and he was sucking in deep breaths.

"I gotta show you something," Oliver said.

"Show me what?"

"Will you just hurry up and get down here."

CHAPTER 3

"Oh God, Oliver, why would you show me that?" Brian said, pulling his tee shirt over his nose to mitigate the stench.

"Because I needed somebody else to see," Oliver said.

"How did you even find this, or did you—"

"Why would I kill a deer? And with what?"

"I don't know; I'm just trying to figure it out."

"Me too. Look, though. There is no blood. No injuries or anything."

"Maybe it had a heart attack or something. It is really big. Like the size of a moose."

"Maybe. I was just taking the woods shortcut from the basketball court and saw it lying here," Oliver said, stepping closer.

"Don't touch it."

"I'm not. Just looking," Oliver said and did the complete opposite.

He reached down and stroked the large antler shooting from the skull of the elk.

"I thought you weren't gonna—"

"Feel this," Oliver said, and Brian backed away.

"Let's just go back to my place and we can throw around the football and forget this even—"

"That's all we ever do. Don't you want some adventure in your life? I thought you would think this was cool. I guess I was wrong. Why don't you throw it around with your dad?"

Oliver stormed off. The remaining leaves from autumn's past rusted under his feet.

They lived in the same direction, but Brian waited until Oliver was out of sight before he made his way up to his bedroom.

He slammed the door harder than he wanted. He expected his dad to shout, but nothing came. Brian buried his face into his mattress until he heard a car outside.

Brian rose from his bed and walked past his broken dresser with his jeans, sweatpants, tee shirts, and underwear spilling out of the drawers. He considered forgetting the vehicle and picking up the Nintendo Gameboy and having a run of *Super Mario Bros*, but the shouting that began outside held his attention.

He pressed his face against the cold windowpane so he could get the angle of Alaina's driveway. She was flailing her arms and shouting something at her father that was too muffled to hear.

Alaina went inside her home, and Brian could hear her footfalls ascending. He moved to the right and out of view. He swiped the disposable camera sitting to the right of his PlayStation and used his thumb to move the dial. It made a mechanical cranking sound, so the camera knew it was time for a new photo.

Brian peered over the windowsill. Alaina had entered her room and splashed onto her bed just as Brian did after his strange argument with Oliver.

Now, Brian would wait for Alaina. Just watch and wait.

CHAPTER 4

After a boring Sunday of video games and no word from Oliver—his dad said he went straight to his room and hadn't seen him since, when Brian called. Brian was asleep earlier than he ever had been. Oliver was his whole life, and without him it was boring. Maybe he should have been more interested in what his best friend was going on about. He would talk to him in school the next day.

On Monday morning, Brian saw Oliver rooting through his own locker as if it didn't belong to him. Textbooks, notebooks, a bagged lunch were falling to the ground.

"Looking for something?" Brian asked.

Oliver peered from behind the blue locker door. He looked different. He looked horrible. Bags were heavy under his eyes. His skin was pale, and his body odor wafted into Brian's nostrils. Brian was immediately concerned.

"Oh my God, are you okay, Oli?" Brian hadn't called him his nickname in years.

"I'm fine, Brain, just leave me to my thing, okay?" Oliver said, his voice muffled in the enclosed space. Brian felt a small sense of relief when Oliver called him the silly nickname Oliver had for him. It showed Brian his best friend was still his normal self. He hoped.

Brian was going to continue his speech of concern when his eye caught Alaina strutting down the hall. She walked with confidence and intensity. Not in a way where she was full of herself, but having some confidence wasn't a bad thing.

When she stopped to turn the combination into her locker, her dark red manicured nails twisting the lock, Brian was overcome with excitement. A yellow plaid skirt today; she must've had a closet full. One of each color. Brian took her exchange of books before class as an opportunity to approach.

The other kids in the hall who were horseplaying and scrambling to class were a blur to Brian. All that mattered was Alaina.

His heart was a non-stop pitter patter against his rib cage. His heart was bursting for a girl he never said a word to. His feelings were strictly cosmetic. He knew nothing of her personality or what she enjoyed. He just knew he needed to be with her.

"You live next door to me, right?" Brian couldn't believe those words trickled from his mouth so perfectly.

"Oh, yeah," she said and turned back to her locker.

He blew it already. She wouldn't want to go out with a lanky, pimply kid whose Saturday nights were spent—what this weekend would be—on his seventy-fifth hour of *Pokémon: Red*. Brian viewed himself as a loser because that was what he was.

"Yeah," Brian said. He remained in that spot. His mind was blank. What else did he say to a pretty girl? When he talked with Oliver, he felt like he could talk for hours without stopping.

Alaina gave Brian a side-glance stare.

Brian opened his mouth to speak when Oliver went by with a stack of books in his arms, nearly spilling them when he bumped Brian from behind.

"Geez, Oliver, watch where you're going," Brian said. But Oliver continued down the hall and around the corner.

"He seems a little weird today," Alaina said.

It took Brian a second to recognize she was talking to him.

"You're friends with him, right?" Alaina said.

"Oh, yeah. He's definitely been acting strange. Even this weekend."

"What happened over the weekend?"

Brian couldn't believe it. A real conversation with a real girl.

"Well, he showed up at my house and—"

The bell birred overhead.

"Sorry, I'm late for class," Alaina said, gathered the books she needed, and scurried out of sight, leaving Brian in the deserted hallway. Alone again.

CHAPTER 5

Brian stepped off the school bus, his bookbag in his hands due to the weight of the books he was carrying. Mondays was homework day from all the teachers. Like they all came together to torture their students on the worst day of the week.

He needed to walk another mile and a half to get home. It wasn't cold, spring was swinging in nicely, but the Starter jacket made it that much more comfortable for Brian.

When he swung onto Shady Street, he held a moment of sadness. Oliver was usually right next to him for the walk home. When Brian saw he wasn't on the bus, his stomach dropped. After seeing him acting weird in the halls and during the classes they shared, Brian's alarm bells were sounding. When Brian tried communicating with him, Oliver pushed him away. He wished he knew what happened to his best friend.

However, there was somebody next to him on this trip to his home. Alaina kept her distance, but when she typically got off with Brian and Oliver, she was always ten feet behind them. Today, she stayed six feet apart, but side by side.

"Are you worried about your friend?"

The words made Brian jump. He wasn't expecting her to initiate conversation.

"Uh, oh, yeah. I don't know where he is."

"Should we tell his dad? He will probably be worried sick if he doesn't come home."

When Oliver's mom died at the beginning of last school year, the school held a memorial service in the gymnasium. Oliver said he thought it was nice of the school. Brian saw it as exploiting personal information to an entire school.

We. She called them a "we."

"I don't know. Maybe he's walking home. He did that after we got into a fight one time. I borrowed his comic book. His favorite comic book and spilled milk on it. He didn't talk to me for a whole month. But, yeah, it's not a super far walk. Maybe he's doing that." Brian was sweating. He was rambling. He sweated and rambled when he was nervous.

"Maybe. But I still think his father should know how strange he was acting. I'm gonna do it," Alaina said and started for Oliver's home.

Brian followed.

Alaina knocked on the wood door, and Brian stood five feet back on the walkway.

They waited a full minute before Alaina knocked again. No answer. No movement of any kind.

"Maybe he's not home," Brian said.

"The car is in the driveway," Alaina said and knocked again.

Brian knew Mr. Jones's pickup truck was sitting a few feet to his right, but he might have gone for a walk or gotten a ride someplace.

Still nothing.

"Maybe we could wait and see if maybe he comes home, then we can ask him what's up," Brian suggested.

"Maybe," Alaina said, but she was distracted.

She stepped off the front stoop and walked up the driveway to the right. Brian could see his house through the shrubbery making its way back to a nice green color. He stopped. There was something extra in his driveway. A beige covering. A car.

When his attention was diverted back to Alaina, she was standing on a garbage can, peeking into the Jones's home.

"What are you doing?" Brian said, rushing to make sure she didn't fall from the shaky can.

"Just seeing if there's anything suspicious. It's not illegal unless you go inside."

Brian couldn't conclude that as a fact or not, but he knew in his gut that they shouldn't be peeking inside others' homes. Even those of a best friend. The Jones's considered Brian part of the family, but still, others' privacy was their own.

Alaina hopped down. Her baby-blue bookbag was lighter than his black knapsack. Did she have less homework than him? A strange thought in a time like that.

Alaina rounded to the back yard. "Look," Brian said, pointing to his own home. He wanted to divert Alaina from doing any further detective work before they were in an interrogation room answering questions from a real detective about why they were breaking and entering.

"That car wasn't there when I left for school this morning," Brian said.

"Oliver doesn't drive a car," Alaina said flatly.

"Yeah, but it's something different. It could lead to a clue about where Oliver could be."

Alaina nodded in agreement.

They crossed over yards through the branches, scraping against their faces and clothes uncomfortably.

"Lift the cover off," Alaina said, observing the shape under the beige cover anybody would pick up as a vehicle.

Brian was nervous to see what was underneath. His dad suggested he was getting a new car, but his dad was at work. His car was missing from the driveway.

Brian lifted the cover, revealing two bug-eye headlights and a silver metal front grill staring at him. Alaina was on the opposite side, helping with the reveal. The long red hood. The shining silver rims holding the tires. The white interior blinding them from the sunlight bouncing off its color. The convertible top tucked away in the back just in front of the cherry red trunk. It was a gorgeous vehicle.

"Did your dad get a new car?" Alaina asked.

"I think he might have."

"Your dad got that car for his son."

Brian jumped. He turned up at the side door to see his father lurking behind the screen. Alaina dropped the cover to the floor.

His dad exited. "An old player of mine, Richard Mayland, actually one of the best wide receivers I ever had the pleasure to coach. Played for a Division One team. Anyway, he called me and offered five hundred dollars to take it off his hands."

"Is that good?" Brian asked.

"Good? The first thing I asked was, 'what's wrong with it?'"

"And does it turn on?" Brian asked.

"It does much more than that. It is in perfect working order with one thousand miles on the odometer."

"Wow," Alaina said, then popped a cupped hand over her mouth.

"Aren't you going to introduce me to your friend here?" his dad said.

"Oh, yeah, this is Alaina; she lives next door."

"Yeah, I spoke with your dad the other day. He knows his football, that guy."

Alaina nodded. "Yes, sir. He wanted me to be the first female to play in the NFL, but I couldn't get the throwing or catching or kicking down, so he gave up on that dream a long time ago."

"Well, I'm sure you did great. And I'm sure a woman will come along within the next twenty years or so and enter the professional level. It will be a sight to witness."

"Thank you," Alaina said. "I hope so."

"Now, son. Richard Mayland did say something about this car that made me uneasy, but I think it's a bunch of bologna. He told me this car is evil."

Alaina and Brian couldn't hold back their smiles and broke into bouts of laughter.

"I had the same reaction when he said that," Brian's dad said. "But when you put together the pieces. The low mileage and perfect condition for a car thirty-plus years old. I just can't imagine why the owners would want to get rid of something so perfect so quickly after getting it. I drove it back from the lot where Richard left it, and all was fine."

Alaina and Brian looked at one another, starting to understand. "So, you're giving it to me?" Brian asked.

"Yeah," his dad said, a sigh of self-contempt. "He, Richard, said nobody's ever died in it or anything. He assured me again and again that it is perfectly safe. All he said was weird things happened inside. Things he didn't want to talk about. Things he said were 'personal.' He said it was as if the car had known him his whole life."

This sent shivers down Brian's back.

"But he assured me it is safe to drive, and it would be great for you as a first-time driver. Simple automatic transmission and fun to operate. But, if anything happens, even something minor, I need you to let me know, okay?"

Brian was staring at his father.

"Okay?" his dad said again, agitation growing.

"Okay. I will. Thanks, Dad," Brian said and embraced him.

"Hey, son. Not in front of the girl."

Alaina giggled as Brian shot his hands behind his back.
They all shared a laugh.
A laugh that was short-lived.

CHAPTER 6

Oliver was missing.

He never showed up at home Monday night, and his father called the police. The police showed up and told Mr. Jones that they couldn't begin the investigation until he was missing for twenty-four hours. Twenty-four hours later, an officer was knocking on Brian's front door to speak with him.

"Did you notice anything odd or strange about his behavior the last time you saw him?" the officer, a large man who could barely fit in their kitchen chair, asked.

"No, I mean, yes, he was acting strange," Brian said.

"Strange how?"

"Well,"—Brian paused to glance at his father, who was observing from behind the portly cop—"he looked like he didn't sleep for a long time. He had those bags under his eyes. He smelled bad. And he looked like he was late for something, but not like the class he was going to, more like something important. During class, he didn't participate; he just laid his head on his desk and slept. That's not like him."

The cop jotted some notes down and scratched the beard stubble on his chin. "And you didn't see him when school ended?"

"We always meet out front of the school and get on the bus together. The driver was yelling for me to get on because I was looking around past the other kids, but I couldn't find Oliver. So, I just got on the bus and left. I should've stayed, shouldn't I? This is my fault."

Brian felt the tears start in his throat and work their way to his eyes.

"No, of course not. Son, what were you going to do? If he ran away or—" His dad stopped. "Something else happened. It is beyond your control."

"Your father is correct. Whatever the reason, it lays on Oliver and only Oliver," the cop said.

Brian wiped the single tear from his cheek as the cop rose from the creaking chair and shook Brian's hand.

"If there's anything else you remember, and I mean anything at all. You'd be surprised how the smallest information can have the largest impact on these types of cases," the cop said and handed a business card to Brian along with one to Brian's dad.

"We'll find him. One way or another. We always find them." The cop's parting words stuck with Brian. They weren't comforting, but Brian knew the coming days were going to be very far from comfortable.

CHAPTER 7

Brian didn't lay a finger on his new car until four days after his initial touch. He couldn't fathom cruising around town with the top down and not have Oliver in the passenger seat next to him.

When he did touch it that Friday, it was the evening Alaina walked into his bedroom. He was spread out on his bed, mindlessly button-mashing his Nintendo Gameboy. The woman of his dreams creaked open the door with the sign clearly stating "No others allowed" taped to the front.

"Hey, Brian," she said, her voice so sweet.

"Brian, your friend Alaina is here. I sent her upstairs. Don't do anything I wouldn't do," his father called from downstairs.

Luckily, Brian decided on pants and a shirt for his relaxation time. Any other day he might have been caught in his unflattering undies.

"Oh, shoot. Sorry for the mess," Brian said, frantically throwing clothes into his hamper and covering up any carpet stains from the drinks he wasn't supposed to bring into his room that spilled.

"That's fine. I'm just getting tired of sitting around doing nothing," Alaina said.

Brian nodded, sitting back on his bed. He was in a dizzy spell from rushing around to clean and having a pretty girl so close to where he was most vulnerable. "We can't really do anything."

"We have to try at least," Alaina said, her eyes glimmering. Not like she was about to cry but glimmering with worry and hope.

"What would we do?" Brian asked.

"Is there any place you can think of that Oliver would go to just chill? A place where he would go to just get away from everything?" Alaina asked.

Brian was stumped. There were places they would go together. The comic shop, Blockbuster, McDonalds when they were hungry, and the movie theater when they were excited for a new release. When they were on their own, Oliver would mostly be next door doing similar activities as Brian would do. Then Brian peered down at the PlayStation, and his mind hatched an idea.

"I think I know where he could be," Brian said.

He snatched the keys to his new ride off the counter and headed out the door.

CHAPTER 8

As soon as Brian started the engine, his brain dropped into a momentary lapse. A flash of Oliver. Blood smeared on his face or was it the fruit punch he enjoyed so much? Either way, he snapped back to his driveway and the car.

The smooth white leather seats felt cool under Brian. The interior red stitching was precise and looked virtually untouched, as with the rest of the car. The center armrest was a joy to rest his forearm on as he placed his hands on ten and two on the steering wheel that was larger than he was used to and backed out of the driveway.

"So, you never told me where we are going," Alaina said from the passenger seat. She needed to raise her voice over the roaring engine.

"Harry's," Brian said.

"The arcade downtown?"

Brian nodded. "There was one day Oliver was feeling down after his mom passed away. I tried everything to cheer him up. He said he just wanted to be by himself. Afterwards, he told me he walked the three miles to Harry's and was there for three hours until he was kicked out. He told me he forgot all about his mom's passing and it was the place he would go when he was upset. It was his comfort place. He has to be there."

"Aren't they closed now?" Alaina asked.

Brian peered down at the digital clock on the old-fashioned dashboard. It read 5:37 p.m. "In about twenty minutes. But I'm not worried if they're open or closed. He will be there no matter what."

Alaina nodded as if she understood perfectly what Brian meant. "What about you?"

"What?"

"Where is a place you go or something you do that brings you comfort? I know your mama died too."

Brian nodded and peered down at his lap while rolling to a stop sign. "Oliver. Oliver is my comfort," Brian said with a glimmer in his eye. And unlike Alaina, Brian was beginning to cry.

CHAPTER 9

Harry's was tucked into a strip mall between a laundromat and Brian and Oliver's favorite comic shop. There were adults moving in and out of the various clothes and entertainment stores while Alaina and Brian entered Harry's minutes before they closed.

A few kids were playing *Space Invaders*. A couple others were button-mashing the *X-Men* arcade game. The teenage associate sat behind the glass counter sporting toys and gag gifts to choose from when enough tickets were won from the machines.

Brian and Oliver dreamed of saving enough for the Nintendo 64. Oliver kept their combined ticket winnings in a shoebox under his bed. They were still three thousand tickets short, but they had the drive and determination to get it done. Brian hoped they would still be able to.

It was the same emotion he needed to find Oliver. The basketball game was empty. The Skee-Ball was vacant. Oliver's favorite, *Street Fighter II* was just as deserted.

"We close in five minutes. Please make your way to the exit. Thank you," the skinny associate said in a monotone voice and walked back to his place behind the counter.

"I don't think he's here," Alaina said.

Brian was thinking the same. But he did have one more place to check.

Brian took off to the rear of the arcade. Between *Space Invaders* and *Pac-Man* was a door that read "Emergency Exit Only – Alarm Will Sound."

"Hey, you can't go out—"

The associate's calls were cut off by the door slamming behind Alaina and Brian. No alarm sounded. The alley behind the store led out to Main Street and was narrowed by a chain link fence. But it was empty other than a single milk crate where the teenage worker inside probably sat to smoke during his breaks.

Brian fell to the floor. He lost all hope. He was sure he would find Oliver at his favorite location.

Alaina sat next to him and put an arm around his shoulders. He didn't panic or feel any excitement from a girl touching him. It only felt like it supposed to be that way. He remembered a short time of his parents being together. Being in love. Brian wanted that. While the other boys in his class were wanting to go to bed with other girls, Brian wanted to be in a home with one. With Alaina.

Brian dropped his head onto her shoulder and said, "Let's go back to the car and figure out a plan B."

Once Brian stuck the key into the ignition and the engine came alive, he was struck by a mental image. Not just an image but a video playing in his mind. A dream, he thought.

He was wandering through the forest. Trees sprouted around him. Leaves returned to their rightful place on branches. The sun's rays glimmered through the tree arms. Oliver was in front of him, lying in the ground. He rested next to an elk. The animal was hollow. No guts. No nothing. Only skin and bones keeping it together. Oliver sat up. He looked the same as he had in the flash he had back when he first started the car. The outline of his mouth was stained with red. "What have you done?" Brian asked.

"Help me," Oliver called in return. Then the ground began to shake. An earthquake for the ages. Brian was falling when he opened his eyes and Alaina was hovering over him in the car.

"What happened?" Brian asked.

"I don't know. You started the car and then you were staring straight ahead, muttering words I couldn't understand."

"I think I understand," Brian said.

"Did you see something?" Alaina asked.

"Yes. And I'm positive I know where Oliver is."

CHAPTER 10

On the way back toward their houses, Brian was tasting something fruity on his lips. He peered over to a now shy Alaina.

"Did you kiss me?" Brian asked.

For the first time Brian saw a redness in her high cheekbones. "I didn't know what else to do. I was shaking you and you weren't snapping out of it, so—yes, I kissed you."

Brian couldn't help but smile and give off a blush of his own.

"Can you do it again when I'm awake?" Brian asked.

"Well, maybe—"

"Oh, shoot," Brian said, looking forward and into the face of an elk. He slammed on the brakes and the car skidded to a stop.

"What? What happened?" Alaina asked.

Brian took a second to get his breathing back as he watched the deer jog into the woods. "You didn't see that big—"

Brian saw the basketball court Oliver would frequent, flipped the transmission into park, and exited the vehicle.

"Where are you going? We're in the middle of the street."

"Oliver is in here."

Brian ran until he couldn't run any longer. He knew the path and how it would lead him out and spill him into his own back yard. Alaina, the track athlete, was keeping pace and eventually caught up with Brian.

"What's going on?" she asked.

"Oliver took me into the forest the day before he went missing to show me something. It was a deer. A big deer. And in my vision, I saw him—you didn't just see it run in front of the car?"

Alaina shook her head.

Before any of that could be sorted out, this was it. The deer was there on its side. The beautiful antlers poking from its head. Its guts poking from its hind legs. A river of blood flowing into the dirt.

Then a squeal. A primal screech like a car's worn belt crying for oil. Oliver leapt from a tree. His clothes were torn. His face was covered in scrapes. That red goatee plastered on his face.

"Oliver," Brian said. Joy and relief were absent from his face as he studied the kind of conditions his best friend appeared to be living in. "Everybody's been looking for you."

Oliver stared for a long time before he picked a small branch shaved at one end into a point.

Brian looked over at Alaina, and he could tell they were thinking the same thing.

"Get back to the car."

They ran with Oliver on their tail. Oliver took some swipes with his stick weapon and even threw it like a javelin. It stuck in a tree trunk inches from Alaina's head. Alaina squealed but didn't stop running.

Freedom and relief. Brian didn't bother opening the door. He leapt into the driver's seat and started it up.

Once the car was running, he watched as Oliver stopped at the edge of trees, dropped his weapon, and held his palms to his ears. As Alaina entered, Brian revved the gas, and it caused Oliver to roll around in what looked like pain.

"We need to go, Brian," Alaina said.

And that was what they did.

CHAPTER 11

"What is going on?" Alaina asked.

"I wish I knew," Brian said.

"Should we call somebody and tell them we know where he is?" she said.

"If he attacked us like that, then the police wouldn't stand a chance. They would shoot him before he had time to throw his stick."

The car was off and around the corner from their houses. Brian didn't want his dad looking out the window. There would need to be an explanation Brian couldn't give for returning after the time he was supposed to be in bed. Even on a Friday night. And Brian feared the situation needed a resolution tonight.

"He was affected by the sound of the car," Brian said.

"But what does that mean?" Alaina asked.

"I don't know. I wish I knew what was going on inside his head. The car has been affecting me sometimes, so maybe he is seeing stuff too." Brian's head was spinning with possibilities. The response came out stronger than he expected.

"Maybe we can go back without the car and then we can maybe talk to him," Alaina said.

"No, that probably won't work; just let me think."

Alaina furrowed her brows and turned, looking into a home with the news on a TV. "I'm just gonna go home."

"No, I need you," Brian said.

"Clearly you don't. This is between you and your friend. And he tried to kill me, so I've had enough for tonight. I am just so tired."

Brian was outside of his mind. With the stress of his best friend missing and the strain over the day's events, he grabbed Alaina by her cheeks, soft to the touch, and pressed his lips against hers. Surprisingly, she didn't pull away or run for her life. She opened her mouth and slid her tongue across Brian's. Maybe she needed to de-stress just as Brian did.

They continued the make-out session for a few more minutes, with Alaina even allowing Brian under her shirt to run his hand along her midriff.

They were interrupted by the start of the engine.

"Why did you turn it on?" Alaina asked.

"I didn't. It just did by itse—"

Then the air conditioning cut on full blast, cooling down their hot and heavy activity, but it was too cold on a not-exactly-warm night. Even with the convertible top and windows back up.

"Turn it off," Alaina said.

But Brian was turning the dials. Blue to red. On to off. The air continued to blow. Then a fluttering sound. Like a playing card in the spokes of a bicycle tire to make it sound like an engine.

Cards fluttered out of the car's vents. There were hundreds of little squares covering Alaina. She had a blanket of photos on her. She picked one up and placed her hand over her mouth. Brian picked up one of his own. His blood ran icy. How was that possible? They were inside the roll of film inside the camera sitting on his dresser.

"Never talk to me again. I cannot believe I actually liked you, creep."

Before he could open his mouth to protest, Alaina was out of the car and out of his life forever.

He tore the polaroid picture he had taken of Alaina undressing in her bedroom and watched the pieces float to the car's rug.

CHAPTER 12

Brian parked the car in the driveway and waited another hour before he walked inside his house. He needed to get out any tears and anger he had lingering in his system before facing his dad.

"Do you know what time it—"

He must've seen it in Brian's face. The defeat.

Brian dropped the key into his father's palm and said, "Bring it back. Wherever you got that thing, take it back or give it to somebody else. It has no place for me. Or you. Just get rid of it."

Brian marched up the stairs, and once at the top he said, "I'll ground myself. Sorry, Dad."

He slammed the door and because curiosity was a human condition, he peeked toward the window that ruined a friendship and more. It was closed, and a shade Brian had never seen before blocked any view into her bedroom. It was to be expected, but it still caused an insanely deep uncomfortable feeling in the pit of his stomach.

He picked up the camera, opened the back, and removed the film. Then he opened his dresser drawer. At the bottom was a Zippo lighter Oliver found one day and decided it was the perfect gift for the non-smoker who feared fire.

Brian flicked it open and pulled the wheel, triggering the flame. He stared at it. It wasn't so scary. Flashes in his mind returned. The elk on its side. Oliver unable to leave that space. Oliver using the animal as his only food source. Why was he trapped there?

He held the flame under the film until it melted to a plastic slab of nothing. The smell was sure to alert his dad to something, but Brian didn't care. All he could think of was that car and Oliver.

Oliver didn't act in that strange way until that car came along. The day he was acting strange was the day it was sitting in the driveway.

Brian sat up and snapped the lighter shut. He walked downstairs. His dad was snoozing in his recliner, and Brian slipped out of the side door. He opened the shed in the back yard and removed a can of gasoline. He carried it to the front and dumped the liquid all over the car's exterior and interior. The rancid smell poked into Brian's nose. Brian figured his dad would let the car sit in their driveway for at least the entirety of the upcoming summer, and that was far too long.

Brian flicked the lighter and tossed it into the passenger seat. The orange and blue flames covered the evil thing in seconds. Brian stood and watched for a minute. He knew the neighbors would be on their stoops to view the flaming car and talk about it for years to come.

As Brian was entering the front door to let the vehicle burn out, the car started on its own again. Then it moved. It went into reverse, then straightened itself so the googly eye headlights were facing Brian. It revved, and then the tires squealed, shooting directly for Brian. He was too in shock to move.

Moments before the ball of flame hit Brian, Brian was tackled from the side. Somebody was on top of him. He watched the car hit the front stairs. The cement crumbled and flames caught the siding of his home. The home his father worked so hard for on his own. And now he was inside sleeping. He hoped the noise and fire alerted him enough to escape.

"Dad," Brian yelled.

"He'll be okay," Oliver reassured him. And within seconds his dad was coming down the driveway, coughing up any smoke that entered his lungs.

"Dad," Brian said again and hugged him.

The neighbors rushed from their homes, including Alaina and her father, Mr. Jefferson with a comforting hand on Alaina's shoulder.

"Oli," Brian said. "You're back." There was a hug for his best friend too. He made eye contact with Alaina, but she quickly turned away. "What happened?"

"It's a long story, but just know you did the right thing, Brain."

Brian could hear the sirens echoing in the distance as his home and the car were being turned to a charred, blackened mess.

He had who was important to him.

Brian had friends and family.

The love he was searching for came with sadness and pain.

He knew that perfectly well now.

For R.L. Stine.

What our Minds Once Were

When I was a little girl, the teachers said I had the smartest brain they had ever seen of all their students. Quick-witted, educated, and well-mannered at seven years old was refreshing for her teachers; at least that's what my momma told me.

As I aged, so did my brain. My teen years were exceptional meeting my loving husband at a drive-in theater. I went with my best friend Marilyn to see *Strangers on a Train*, which Marilyn wanted to see. I hoped for *Alice in Wonderland*, but I was told to grow up. Although I was grown, nearly eighteen and completing high school in a matter of months. One thing I wanted as I grew older was to keep that spark of childhood inside me forever.

After the movie completed and I was sufficiently terrified, which was an easy thing to do, the older generations would exit the drive-in, leaving the teens who would play tunes from their cars. We were in Marilyn's bright blue station wagon, and she played rock n roll tunes, a new wave of music that wasn't allowed in my momma and dada's house. I was stern and cold when Marilyn got out and jumped onto the hood, shaking her hips and moving her arms in a swinging motion to the beat of the drums.

Embarrassment crept up my body, coloring my face a dark red. Embarrassed for my friend until a man hopped on the car with her and they were holding hands, swaying to the music. Marilyn's long blue dress swung prettily while the man in a button down with suspenders hooked onto slacks raised her arms and she twirled like the princess I wished to be. My shyness kept me from many things, and my friend was fearless. If being fearless got her to hold hands with a handsome slicked back gentleman, then I was ready to break free from my introverted shell.

I climbed onto the hood and stepped on my floor-length dress. Fear struck as I stepped on the hem of my dress and fell to the floor before my hand was yanked and pulled close to the boy who had freed Marilyn from their dance.

"Almost took a bad spill there," the boy said.

"I did almost, didn't I," I said with the English language I was well versed in, not connecting in my dizzying head.

"What are you doing after this tonight?" he asked.

Marilyn was driving her car, and both of our parents had a strict curfew that expired in just a few hours.

"Well, I need to—"

"Go to the roller rink for a shake," Marilyn interrupted me from telling the boy I was required home at a certain time.

"Well, I'll meet you there, then…"

He was waiting for my name, and I sputtered out, "Delores, but my friends call me Maggie."

"Where does Maggie come from Delores?" he asked.

"Maggie…Margaret is my middle name," I said.

"Well, Maggie Margaret, I will see you at the roller rink in fifteen."

On the way downtown, fifteen minutes in the opposite direction from our homes, we never once discussed curfew or being nervous about being punished; it was all about the boy on the hood of the car.

"You two are getting married, I can feel it," Marilyn said. "The way you looked into each other's eyes was magical."

"You met him first. I don't want to steal him away or anything of the sort."

"Oh please. He is all yours, and besides, when you find the man of your dreams, don't let him go."

Of course, Marilyn meant none of those words as the years went by and my love only grew stronger for him. Marilyn separated herself further and further from me.

It began the night at the rink when he finally told me his name was Charles, and he was the one who taught me to skate. Before that night, I had been to the roller rink twice and had the skates on for ten minutes each time after falling and growing frustrated both times. But Charles held my hand and guided me around in circles, working on my balance and confidence. We went around what must've been over thirty times. Marilyn sat at the table on the outside of the rink, and with each pass by, her smile faded into a frown, as we went around until we were kicked out. But the reason for resentment from Marilyn was when Charles wrapped his arm around my waist and pulled me close, locking his lips to mine. My princess moment had arrived, and I was in the world of Charles from that moment forward. On the way home that night to our punishment of one week grounded, Marilyn didn't say one word until we pulled up to the front of my home.

"I don't mean to make you upset," I said.

"I'm not upset. You just don't need to go around shoving your happiness in my face."

"I'm sorry, but if you can't be happy for your friend, then we shouldn't be friends at all."

I hadn't meant what I said, but Marilyn drove off, and I was ignored in the halls of school and any chance meetings outside. She went off to college three states away, and I stayed in town for university. It was the plan all along, and our separation as friends was inevitable. But Charles was the perfect replacement.

The college years were the best of my life. Charles attended a separate university but was an hour's drive away. Fashion design was my passion from the first time I saw a dress on the racks in the department store as a child. The fabric, layers, and designs were fascinating to learn and create. Sewing classes, art classes, and math classes consumed my time at the university. There was always something to create, and it was the most fun I had in my life up to that point.

Charles met me at my dorm each Friday with flowers in one hand and my favorite chocolates in the other. I told him all the candy would make me fat, and he said, "You're perfect now and you will always be perfect." I was living in a fantasy world. Just like the books I read where the princess finds her prince to take her back to his castle and live happily ever after.

College graduation was when that fantasy became reality. We moved into a house on the countryside; ten miles separated us and our closest neighbors. It was silent and it was glorious.

With my new degree in fashion and a sewing machine bought for me as a birthday present by Charles, I was ready to be the next great designer and couldn't wait to see my designs hanging on the racks inside Macy's and Filene's stores like I had seen when I was a child.

After completing thirteen different designs including eight dresses, three blouses, and two pairs of shoes, I was ready to use Charles's car to drive into the city and pitch to the stores to sell my creations.

I never got to complete my dream, as in the days before I was set to meet with the store managers, I fell ill and couldn't hold food inside. One visit to the doctor, and Charles and I were overcome with emotion when we were told we were going to have a baby.

There was no convincing Charles that I still wanted to go present my designs, but he insisted I stay at home and rest. He was scared, I could tell, that something could potentially happen to the baby or me. He saw it as protecting me, and I saw it as keeping me locked up inside away from my dreams.

Meanwhile, the farming business Charles created right outside our doorstep was booming, and in the nine months the baby grew, so did our finances. An entire room with a crib, wallpaper, a chest filled with toys, and a new floor was set for baby Declan to have the most comfortable life moving forward.

As the seasons flew by and the crops were putting food on the table and money in our pockets, I grew fond of the idea of being a full-time mother. Although the closet door had to remain closed. I couldn't bear to see the designs I worked so hard on for years were collecting dust.

Motherhood proved to be rewarding. Seeing Declan's face each morning and getting bigger with each blink while another grew inside me felt like an accomplishment all on its own. But, with each passing day, the joys of childhood and my dreams were slowly slipping away. Getting older as a teen was exciting: wondering what each day would bring and ready to take it on. Now, as the days passed, the memories of the times of joy depleted.

Charles was out when Sandy was looking to be welcomed into the world. The pain of childbirth with no medical intervention, and lying in a bathtub with nobody around to assist, and a crying three-year-old in the adjacent room was the most terrifying experience of my life. Five hours Charles was gone before he walked into the bathroom and surely saw a woman ready to give in. He caught the baby and rushed both of us to the hospital an hour away. I was determined to be fine, but Sandy was having complications. She was in the NICU for three weeks before she was released to us. And she was beautiful. Dad's blue eyes and Mom's peach skin were signs she would grow into a wonderful woman one day.

The older I got, the quicker time zoomed by. It was almost as if the universe was punishing me for aging. Living vicariously through my children was what brought me joy over those vanished years. Declan's first day of preschool turned into his high school graduation. Sandy's first steps turned into receiving her driver's license. When Declan went off to college across the country and Sandy turned from a momma's girl to a bratty teen not behaving was when the decline of my own life began. Charles was out on the farm for twelve hours every day, and when he came to bed, he barely said two words to me. The three most important human beings in my life had shut me out, and all that I had in my life was raising those kids and doing whatever Charles asked because he held the important piece of my one-third heart; the repayment was a cold shoulder from all, which instantly froze my most important body organ. While receiving something in return was never what I wanted, my self-respect wouldn't allow for disrespect.

One day while Charles was on the tractor tilling the dirt, a responsibility that took hours to complete, I snatched his keys from the hook, threw the dresses, blouses, and shoes I had made twenty years earlier inside, and took off down the road. Downtown had changed since the first time I was expected to meet with the store manager about getting my clothes in the stores. The single small businesses were slowly disappearing and being replaced with monopolies of restaurants and big-name stores. Houses had become tall skyscrapers of selfish money-makers. While I hated the big-name stores, they were the ones I needed to get my clothes on racks. This was not a money-making endeavor; Charles made enough to last us well into our nineties, if the farming economy stayed afloat.

The clothes I made were well past the style of what the current fashion trends were, and each store gave me that same message. Time had gotten away from me, and so had my dreams.

Devastation sat in my chest on the drive home. That pit grew into pain when Charles was standing at the edge of the dirt drive as I pulled onto the property.

"Where did you go off to?" he asked. His dark-haired arms crossed at his chest, his white T-shirt I would need to launder later, and blue overalls were caked in a thick orange-brown dirt. The stomach flutters I had felt holding his hand on the hood of Marilyn's car, and kissing at the roller rink, and the celebration of our wedding day, and seeing how gentle and loving he was to Declan and Sandy vanished with one look. The slicked black hair was a gray-streaked tumbleweed, the soft facial features were rough and hardened, his hazel eyes had darkened to a mean brown under his unkempt eyebrows.

"Just into town," I said. It was my conclusion that he was experiencing the same revelation of the children slipping away and grasping at what life held for us in the remaining years. He had a successful business I wasn't allowed to help with in any way, but my successes always surrounded the children and being a mother. I wanted something too, but it was clear he hated my clothing aspirations.

"I don't remember you asking me to use my truck. Am I wrong?" Charles never hurt me, but I respected his wishes in all our time together, and he treated me with respect in return. I never tested what would happen if I broke that silent agreement between us.

"I just wanted to see—"

"You wanted to see if your little dresses could make you money when I told you I am making you money. All you need to do, all you ever needed to do was make sure the kids were fed, bathed, and loved, but you want to go behind my back, my hard work that I broke my goddamn back doing, and bring in your own income. Is that it?"

"Charles, I just can't sit in that house all day and do nothing."

"That's the problem, you're doing nothing. Sandy is out all hours of the night doing God knows what, and you sit in that rocking chair reading your romance books instead of grounding her and taking some initiative for once."

This back and forth through the window was tiring. I cut the engine off and got out, slamming the door. I gave no rebuttal but instead walked up toward the house. The drive was a mile long, and I was happy for some fresh air.

"So, you're not going to answer me, is that it?" Charles said, following me.

His footfalls were fast, and I could feel him on me. He squeezed my bicep and turned me to face him. "Just like you always do, walk away from your problems," Charles said.

I looked him up and down from his dirty boots to his messy hair and said, "That is exactly what I'm doing." Shoved his arm off me and continued up the drive.

Once inside, I emptied my dresser and closet full of clothes into a suitcase. Charles came in. "What are you doing?"

"Leaving."

"Why, because it's impossible for you to hold a conversation?"

"No, Charles, because all I have ever wanted to do was live my dreams. And before I could do that, you shut them down. You…" I said and poked a finger into his chest. "…told me to stay inside when I helped a little with the farm. You…" I poked him again, and with each step I took forward, he mimicked one backward toward the bedroom wall. "…told me to be a mother to our kids. You singlehandedly killed my dreams. When I want to do one thing, one goddamned thing for myself, you tell me I'm not allowed to do that thing. So, now I'm walking out that door and walking until I find someone who will take me into town."

He was silent for a minute, pacing the room and spilling dirt he would need to sweep up, pondering his next words carefully while I zipped up my suitcase. "And do what, Maggie? Leave your kids without a mother? When Sandy walks through the door and you're gone, what do you think she will do? How will she react when I tell her that her mother abandoned her? And what about Declan? What will happen when I call him and tell him his mother has left for good? And where will you even go?" Before I recognized I was against the wall with Charles breathing into my face, his hand was wrapped around my throat. "Do you think selling your little dresses will be enough to make it on your own?"

"Ch—char—" was all I could get out before swinging my leg and connecting with his testicles. He released his grip, and I ran for the door, but he was faster. He leapt and grabbed my ankle, forcing me to the ground, and he crawled like a demon to get on top of me. Inches from the door and miles from freedom was where I thought I would take my final breath.

But Charles loved protecting his farm. He said the shotgun was for protecting his family, but he never spent over twelve hours every day with his family. That was his problem: he became fixated. He was fixated on my face while he waited for my body to stop moving. I was moving to get closer to the gun leaning on the wall next to the door. I slid closer to the door without him noticing, but he did when the butt of the gun came down hard on the dome of his skull.

The anger left his body, and he was scared.

Good. Feel how I feel for once in your life.

They often say people black out during intense experiences, but I remember pulling the trigger. I never blacked out, but every moment from that life-changing finger pull felt like a dream. An unrealistic fictional world where I died and was positioned into a new place.

His nose disintegrating. His right eyeball melting out of its socket into a creamy soup. His forehead exposing broken skull fragments. His jaw hanging off and dangling like a pendulum. These images were forever in my head. No matter the deterioration of my brain, those images never left me.

Ever.

***

"So, what do we do?" Sandy asked, standing at the foot of the mile-long drive leading up to her childhood house.

"We act normal. She is in a poor state of mind, and whatever you do, do not bring up the far past," Declan said, motioning his sister to begin their walk.

"And what if she brings it up?"

"You have your cell phone?"

Sandy reached into her hoodie pouch and showed the cracked screen as though it were on standby.

"Okay," Declan said. "We have the number for the old folks home downtown. If she gets out of hand, I will bring her back there myself."

"So, why are we not taking your car up the drive in case we need a quick getaway?"

"Jesus Christ, Sandy, this is our mother, not Ted Bundy. And because last time she had to be hospitalized was because she didn't recognize the caretaker walking into her room at the convalescent home and flipped out. I want to do everything I can to not trigger anything in her mind."

His sister nodded and seemed pleased with the response, but ran a finger through her blonde ponytail, setting it on her shoulder, and asked, "What was the conversation like?"

"What do you mean?" he said.

"With the home. Did they find the manuscript and tell you 'Hey, your mom might have killed your father thirty years ago'?"

Declan stopped, they were halfway there, and he stared beyond the wood fence and dead, long forgotten crops that kept them happy through most of their lives. He studied the magenta sky with dusk around the corner. "I never talked to them. When Mom walked out unbeknownst to the place for several hours, they sent an alert to my phone that said she had left and they couldn't locate her. I wasn't worried one bit, though. She always goes back to the same place: here."

Sandy nodded even though she hadn't visited her mother since she was placed inside the home. They never got along. She was a daddy's girl, and his death was what separated her from the family. She was here now because of guilt and, most importantly, wanting to face the person who took away the one she loved the most.

"I sent them an email saying I know where she is, and I will handle it," Declan continued. "In response, they sent me the manuscript. No words in the body of the attached file. It was like they didn't know what to do with the information. Are you sure you don't want to read it, Sand?"

She blew out a breath and said, "Fuck no. Just from what you told me…that was enough."

The old farmhouse hadn't been used as a living dwelling in twenty years. There was no phone, no internet, no bed, not even any ghosts. It was a home that had been squatted and damaged over the years. The front door had ripped off its hinges and lay in the dead lawn. The barn-red color faded and chipped to an ugly shit brown. The white window trim was back to their original wood with the exception of termites feasting on the structure. It looked about ready to collapse, and the goal was to get Mom and themselves out before it did.

"Wow. It looks like shit," Sandy said.

"Long way from running through the fields while Dad planted and soiled, isn't it?"

"We had a good childhood. A happy one for sure. It was during high school when I came home one day, and Dad was—"

Seeing Sandy on her way to tears, Declan said, "Happy memories are what stick around. Just remember that when talking to Mom."

Before stepping inside, the smell was what caught them first. Sandy coughed when the mothball mixed with decaying wood wafted through her senses. Declan panicked as he was readying for a slow introduction to Mom so there were no surprises. The plan was out the window when he heard her call out.

"Who's there? Charles, is that you?"

"No, Mom, it's Declan…and Sandy."

What used to be the living room was bare, and the walls were streaked with a liquid from years past, and the floor was covered in a thick, muddy, unidentifiable substance that was the main source of the stench. Mom stood in the corner of the room staring at the wall and doing something with her hand, but all the siblings could see was her elbow moving vigorously.

"Uh, Mom," Sandy tried.

The snap of Mom's head was so abrupt she feared it would pop off.

"Marilyn? Is that you? I've been meaning to call you about Charles. You can have him back. Never let me live out my dreams."

"No, Mom, it's Sandy. Your daughter."

"Sandy. What grade are you in now? Second or third?"

As sad as Mom had gotten, a twitch of Declan's lip wanted to form a smile.

"They said you left the home, and I just wanted to make sure you were—"

"That retched fucking place wants to keep me in a prison cell, and I told them I'm not going to no prison cell."

The last time Declan saw his mom was when he visited her at the home two years ago. She was at the beginning stages of her mind going downhill but still remembered him and Sandy. Then, her hair was all gray but somewhat healthy, and her skin was loose and patched with blisters and skin tags but well taken care of. Now, it sagged further, and her face was aging like a withered apple. Her hair looked like brittle hay straw.

"Nobody is putting you in any prison," Declan said. "We are here to talk. Remember when you used to read us stories in this room? You would do a different voice for each character."

"I remember that so well," Sandy said. "It was a great memory."

"Pshh. Memories are only a reminder of what could have been," Mom said. "I had so much fun when I was a teen. There was so much hope back then. Dreaming of all that I could accomplish. My world was open to do anything I wanted. Then I met Charles. What a rat that man was. Running away and leaving me alone."

Mom spit at the ground and turned her entire body toward her children. She was holding a knife, a flat, small butter knife. The wall where she stood had a single word carved into the middle. "DED."

"Hey, can I borrow that?" Declan said in a casual way and approached her. Mom gave over the knife with no fight. He stuck it in his back pocket and watched to see what Mom would do next. She stood there in a green dress that stopped at her ankles.

"What does that mean?" Sandy asked. Declan was too surprised that Sandy was asking questions out of her comfort zone to stop the words or steer the conversation differently. "What does D-E-D mean?"

Mom looked back at the wall as though this were her first time seeing the letters. When her gaze came back to the siblings, Declan saw a flicker in her eyes. A moment of clarity, he hoped.

"I don't know," Mom said. Then a tear, one Declan and Sandy read as mental breakthrough, slid down her cheek. "I want to go back."

"Okay, I can take you back to the home. I think that's a great—"

"No." A harsh syllable from Mom. "I want to go back to being fifteen so I can have a do-over. Not just meeting your father but starting things I procrastinated on. Doing things I was too scared or embarrassed to do. Time goes by one second at a time, but it's the years that are faster. If you haven't done something, do it now. Now is the only time."

"Mom, did you kill Dad?"

There was not enough time to take in what Mom had said. Not enough time allotted to stop the words from exiting Sandy's mouth. The flicker in Mom's eyes was gone.

"I didn't kill fucking nobody."

Sandy paused for a second appearing to take a brief mental trip to the past then said, "because I play that day in my head every day. I was out with friends after school. I got home at 6:27. p.m., and the first thing I asked you was where Dad was. You said, 'I don't know. I'm not responsible for him and his actions.' Then the next day I was crying because he still wasn't anywhere to be found. And you said, 'I'm sure he went out. I don't know if he'll be back.' I have played through every scenario in my head when I'm sitting at the dinner table across from my husband and two kids. The smell of bleach was strong for a week. The clothes he wore every day in the field were gone. I looked in his closet."

"Maybe we shouldn't," Declan tried, but Sandy ignored him. And it was unclear if Mom was listening or not. Her dead eyes matched her stiff standing body.

"And remember when I called the police to report him missing a week later without your permission? You didn't like that one bit. But you played your role well. The distraught wife whose husband was working out in the fields and never returned. A different story than the one you told me. I went into town and hung up posters. I went to all the shops he frequented and was worried sick, but you knew where he was the whole time."

Sandy followed Mom's glazed eyes through the non-existent front door and to the fields.

"That's where he is, isn't he?" Sandy asked.

To Declan's surprise, Sandy waited for a rebuttal. One, based on Mom's condition, wasn't coming.

Three full minutes they stood in a circle with nobody speaking but the cawing birds outside.

"Let's go," Sandy said to Declan. Then, before he could say a word she said, "Or do whatever the fuck."

"Mom," he said in a soft, pleading tone. He wanted to know what happened, as he remembered that day, being called to the university office to receive Sandy's call, bawling her eyes out that Dad was missing. Declan came home a week later when no progress was made. And as he stood in the same house thirty years later, progress remained in the same spot.

"Charles, you were a good man. A kind human. Why did you need to kill him?" Mom said and ran for the door. She wasn't fast, but in a moment of instinct, Declan ran after her and held her arm to keep her in the house. To keep his mom safe.

There were no feet under her or anything, but she tripped, and the simultaneous sound of the thud on the floor that had held up better than any other piece of the home and a deafening crack brought Sandy running back inside. Nothing could have prepared the siblings for the guttural, stomach-churning squeal that their hurt mother released to the open fields.

"I can't walk again. I won't be able to," Mom yelled from the side position where it looked as though she thought she was still running, but the use of her legs had become obsolete.

"What did you do, Dec," Sandy said, running up to the front.

"I—I just tried to…"

Before Declan could say more, Sandy had her phone out, dialing 911.

"Should I tell them my brother shoved our elderly mother to the floor?"

"This is not the time."

She was on the phone reciting the address perfectly. Knowing the location so well, they knew help was still a half hour away.

"Then tell me what happened," Sandy said, hanging up the phone.

"My hip is broken. I can't live sitting down for the rest of my days," Mom moaned.

"She took off running and I was trying to—"

"Looks like you succeeded. Now what do we do?"

"What do you mean? We wait for the medics to take Mom to the hospital."

"Where I can rot and die," Mom said.

Seeing Mom in agony, an elderly, frail woman, sent shivers down Sandy's body that ended at her skull, hatching a connection in her mind.

"I think you pushed her, and I will tell the police that," Sandy said, turning away, watching the sunset.

"Why the hell would I do that?"

"You never cared that Dad was missing, did you?"

It felt to Declan like a question out of the blue. He was worried sick about his father being missing, but enough time passed that he knew he wasn't coming back.

"Of course I d—"

"I think you knew he was dead the whole time, and you didn't tell me. You and Mom spent a whole lot of time together way too soon after he was gone. When you came home from college, you didn't have an ounce of worry on your face. It was evident." Sandy said pacing the dirt drive with her fight or flight battling it out.

"Put me out of my misery. I can't live like this," Mom said.

"I just process situations differently than you." Declan said grinding his teeth, a habit ingrained in him since childhood.

"I bet you processed Dad's murder news just fine then. Momma's boy."

"Sandy, where is all this coming from?"

"Where is it coming from? This has been building in my head for thirty fucking years. It's all I think about. It's all I dream about. And the fact that you have always stood there with that stupid blank expression and so easily moved on with your life is where this is coming from."

Declan looked down at his mom and she was sobbing. When Dad was gone, they grew closer. Mom loved to talk back then about her childhood, her teen years, and how she and Dad met. Every detail she remembered down to what they were wearing. She was so sharp.

"You know, as Mom said, he was not good to her," Declan said. "And that's how he will be remembered. And Mom, the crazy lady who snapped and shot him, hiding his body with the crops along with the gun. That's the funny thing about brains; when they begin to lose all sense of reality, it can be a very easy thing to alter." He pulled the knife he took from Mom out of his back pocket.

"Dec, what are you talking about?" Sandy's words were cautious. The shine from the knife caused the three letters Mom carved on the wall to pop into Sandy's head. D-E-D. Declan Everett Dunn.

"The thing about shotguns is they are clunky and tough to carry around," Declan said and pulled a handgun from his rear waistband. "But these are nice and compact."

Sandy raised her hands when the gun was aimed at her. "You can go ahead and run, tell who you want. But unfortunately, Mom has to go." He knelt and pressed the butter knife into Mom's fragile larynx. It burst open with a river of blood within seconds. He placed the knife in her hand. A lifetime of memories completed with watching her own son she brought into this world help her leave it quicker than the snap of a finger.

Sandy was still. She hadn't run away or run toward him. "Good thing she can't murder anyone else, right, Sand?"

"You—you did it."

"Yeah, I wrote the letter on my many visits with Mom. Her mind going was simple enough to even convince her of a murder she never committed. I knew her life better than my own. And with a little fictional freedom, the story became simple."

"Why?" Sandy asked.

"So she could be blamed before she died, and I would be off the hook. Simple."

"No, I mean why did you kill Dad?"

"Because I flew to the university and one month in, they told me I needed to pay tuition. When I called Dad, he said he had done enough for me, and I needed to get a job and pay my own way through college."

"So, you killed him because you needed to work hard?"

"I killed him because he promised to be a father while he was on this earth and he didn't fully deliver. Plus, all you saw was how Dad acted around you, his little girl. He wasn't the perfect man; he was just perfect in your presence."

"And that's why you never had kids, because you would need to provide for them forever?"

"This is not about me."

"This whole thing is about you. We wouldn't be standing in this godforsaken place if it wasn't for you."

Sirens whined, and the medics and police were a mile out.

"Well, congratulations, Sand, it's all yours."

"What are you talking about?"

"When I looked through Mom's and Dad's wills, I get money, a good chunk of change, and you get the farm. And with Mom dead by suicide"—Declan looked back at the doorway as if to confirm—"it's official."

"So why not just say money is the real motivation?"

"Look, sis, we can stand here all night and have a good chat, but I need to kill you so you can start running to make it easier on me."

Declan raised the gun, but Sandy stood her ground. If she was going to die, somebody was going to watch, preferably the emergency services a mile away, or see her blood in the driveway.

"Do you remember when we used to play tag in the big field?" Declan asked.

"Sure," Sandy said, playing along, stalling for time.

"There was one day where you hid behind the corn stalks, and I couldn't find you for hours."

She nodded, remembering.

"I was so worried about you that I ran for Dad and told him you were missing. He ran out the door and found you in less than a minute because you showed yourself when he called your name."

"Okay?" she said.

"I can't wait for when the police, your husband, and your kids are doing the same, but you won't come out because they will walk over your body many times right next to Daddy's."

The lights flashed across the fields, and Sandy knew he was out of time, but while looking at her saviors, a force hit her so hard she had no time to think about balance. Her head bounced off the hard dirt, but she stayed conscious. The second time her head bounced, the world appeared hazy. The third time and her vision was lost, but the sirens were at the front of the driveway. She didn't recall the fourth time.

***

Sandy lost a father she loved so much, a mother she loved so much, and a brother she used to love so much, but what she didn't lose were her memories. After Declan knocked her unconscious, he took off running into the fields that went on for nine miles and cut off in many different directions. When she woke in the hospital with her husband and kids around her bed, she got the news that they hadn't found Declan.

And what she told the police was the whole story. Declan killing their father thirty years ago and their mother yesterday. The officer asked if she knew of any places her brother would have gone. She had to be honest and that other than meeting up yesterday, which was Sandy walking into her own death sentence, she hadn't seen or talked to Declan in fifteen years. He told her he was living by himself in an apartment in New York City and had a job as a software engineer where he was making a ton of money, but she began to realize as she spoke about it how that could be entirely fabricated.

She believed Declan had an anger problem and held that since they were little. He kept it well-hidden, as she never saw any obvious signs, but she always found it odd how he reacted to certain situations. He had no emotions until he was angry. When Declan got angry, his face would become red and his knuckles white. She believed after he wouldn't get financial aid from Dad, he lost his temper, flew home, and shot him in the face with a shotgun. Sandy sat and read the letter Declan wrote. Other than the ending, it was a wonderful story about Mom's life and Dad always being the perfect gentleman from the moment he first laid eyes on her to his last moments.

Mom was a coper. She would push things to the side while she boiled inside. When Dad was gone after she went out for the day, probably to show her dresses, she came home, and he was gone. She coped by not thinking about it and waiting for him to return, especially around Sandy. But Sandy knew when Mom was alone the anxiety would eat her insides and the emotions would flood out.

It was incredible how brains worked and how each human had a separate inner thought process. Sandy liked to think she had a piece of her mom's and her dad's brain. They were interconnected forever in a strange way.

They would find Declan eventually, hopefully before he killed another. But she thought he was done. He thought he would gain from family death; others were not worth it in his mind.

Charles, Sandy's youngest son, and Brad, the oldest, slept on the visitor chairs of the hospital room.

"Are you sure you want caffeinated soda? It's almost bedtime," Greg, her husband, said, returning from the vending machine.

"I'm not sleeping until they catch him, but after that I think my insomnia will be gone."

"Then what should we do all night long?" he said.

"Give me your phone."

He handed over his phone, and Sandy selected a playlist of top songs from the 50s and tapped the shuffle button.

"What are you doing?" he asked.

"Getting up."

"But the doctor said—"

"Give me your hand," she said, with the IV still attached and johnnie coat showing her good stuff to anyone outside the window.

Greg steadied her to her feet as the trumpets and trombones played the sweet harmonies, the quick, steady beat of a drum behind a soulful front man: the beginnings of rock n roll.

"What are we doing?" Greg asked.

Sandy didn't answer, she kept her arms on his shoulders and head on his chest, feet doing a tired two-step, and they swayed to the melody until the sun from the past set over the present dusk connecting three perfect minds together forever.

Remembering Mame.

Edited by: Sara Kelly

Cover Design by: Elderlemon Designs

Joe Baldwin was born and raised in the idyllic state of Connecticut where he received his degree in Criminal Justice. When he is not nose-down in a book you can find him on a long walk beside the roar of traffic or attempting to befriend his pug-tailed tabby cat named Piranha. What our Minds Once Were is his second collection of short stories.